WHERE WE ARE

Free

ISBN 979-8-9883238-2-2 (paperback)
ISBN 979-8-9883238-3-9 (ebook)

WHERE WE ARE

Free

CHRIS GAMBLE

To Mom, now and forever.

JUNE

CHAPTER

ONE

ALMOST HOME.

His bags barely touched the bottom of the trunk before the rideshare driver leaned out the window, looking back at him with a face full of frustration.

"Wait, wait, your stop is on the south side?" the driver asked, pointing to his phone for clarification.

"Yeah, you saw that when you accepted the ride." From the way the driver emphasized the word "south", Dom knew where this was heading. "What's the problem?"

"I'm sorry, I don't go there. I'm canceling. Please, take your bags."

"You what?" Dom tensed. "It's your job to drive people where they need to go. Why pick anyone up from the airport if you're not willing to do that?"

"Sir, please." The driver opened his door.

"Nope, don't waste your energy." Dom dragged his two suitcases and duffel bag out of the trunk.

Still heated by the exchange, his body relaxed once he saw his backup ride pull up to the curb twenty minutes later. The convenience of a rideshare couldn't compare with the feeling of being home, which is what he felt when he saw the black sedan rolling to a stop. He remembered when Kendra's dad finally passed down one of his prized remodeled cars. He wasn't surprised to see it was still in pristine condition.

The passenger window rolled down first, releasing a scream of excitement. Then, a swirl of curly black hair bouncing on the shoulders of a bright pink jacket curved around the hood, carried by swiftly moving white sneakers. "I know it's been a while, Dom, but don't act like you forgot how to greet your best friend!" Her arms spread out wide.

Kendra and Dom were friends since kindergarten, inseparable since bonding over building towers of blocks together. "Of course not," he said as he slid the duffel bag off his shoulder, did their secret handshake, and then embraced her in a hug. "I see you're still keeping all these other artists on their toes," he said, as he noticed the custom designs painted onto the back of Kendra's jacket.

"Can't let 'em get too comfortable," she responded. She flashed a smile, the same one that made it impossible for her to have any enemies. "Come on, hurry up. Gotta get to the *south* side before dark."

Dom shook his head. "Don't even start. I can only imagine what you would have said to the guy."

She looked back, lips pursed, confirming his assumption. "Damn right. But for real, let's go. Traffic plus Maryland drivers. You know how it goes."

He lugged his suitcases into Kendra's trunk, then opened the rear door to throw the duffel bag in. "California traffic is way worse."

"Now you know you were in those books way more than the streets, mister graduate." Kendra pulled off from the airport's pickup area, and headed toward the exit for the highway. Dom laughed, cranking the A/C up on his side. They had only been on the highway for a few miles when the cars began to slow into extended lines. Up ahead, orange cones were guiding people around an accident. "Must have just happened." Kendra hit the steering wheel. "If it's not people driving crazy, then it's all the damn construction slowing the whole city down. We better not get held up too long. You know your mom's cooking up something mean for your grand return."

"Oh, so that's why you agreed to pick me up last minute?" Dom asked. "Wanted to guarantee yourself a plate in return for your graciousness, huh?"

Kendra shrugged playfully. "I mean, if it works, it works."

"S-M-H."

"Look, your mom has been throwing down forever," Kendra said. "Remember how mad I got when you guys would bring your plates of seconds into this car for our ride-arounds? Acting like it was okay to get my seats messy and to not share. S-M-H."

Dom's eyes glanced up at the rearview mirror and into the backseat briefly before his head dropped, resting on the window as he gazed out of it. "Yeah, we were pretty wild back then."

The rows of cars shrunk down to one, inching past the accident before picking up speed again. Kendra cleared her throat to break the silence that spilled throughout the car. "Tell me how finals went. Of course, you graduated and all, but I want the details."

Lucky enough to get a scholarship, Dom left his hometown of Selton City two years ago for a Master's program in counseling out in California. "They weren't too bad. Nothing like freshman year of college when you and I basically didn't sleep for a week trying to cram until the last second. I was more nervous for the exam I had to take to qualify me for my graduate level license. I passed though, so I'm ready," he said, scanning the city's skyline as it came into view.

Dom didn't come from money, so he hadn't been able to come home at all while he was at school. Such a short time, but the city somehow seemed different. The feeling only grew as they left the highway and began driving through the business district.

"Well, I hope it was worth it," Kendra said. "As you can see, things change quickly around here."

GRAND OPENING signs littered the buildings on each side of them and bike lanes took up enough space for the Tour de France to roll through what had once been the most recognizable streets to him. It was a little like coming home to rearranged furniture.

Dom exhaled sharply through his nose. "Here we go again. I told you it would only be two years and then I'd be back for good. Nothing has stopped the plan."

Stopped at a red light, Kendra cocked her head to the side and raised an eyebrow at him. "The plan? That whole fantasy stopped the moment you decided to go to Cali to learn how to talk about feelings."

Kendra may not have had any enemies, but that didn't mean she didn't know how to push buttons.

Dom bit his tongue and squeezed his knees until his fingers hurt. He thought back to the plan he and Kendra made around the time they were starting high school. By their teen years, both were well aware of how the people in their neighborhood were not as well off as the rest of Selton City. They promised each other that somehow, someway they would help their community.

The biggest part of the plan was that they agreed to never leave Selton. Both attended a smaller local college, but once Dom knew he wanted to become a therapist he decided to aim for a top-ranked program. He and Kendra disagreed about his decision from the beginning, but Dom didn't want to talk about it now.

The streets seemed to exhale, growing wider as they left the city proper. Cramped high-rises gave way to more modest-sized buildings and some open plots of land here and there. The people waiting at bus stops along the way gradually changed, too. Skin tones shifted from creams and splashes of caramel to deeper, richer, darker browns. Briefcases became backpacks and custom coffees in hand became sugary sodas.

The minutes dragged until Kendra turned right at a park, bringing into view a wide rectangular sign posted amongst a group of shabby bushes interspersed with white and blue flowers. The four horizontal wooden planks sported chipped dark blue paint and a fading yellow sun, rising above bold white letters that spelled out PARKSIDE. Even as kids, Dom and his friends thought the sign was a weak attempt at making their neighborhood seem more warm and fuzzy than it was. Selton in general gave off a vibe that felt like a façade. Situated right on the edge of debates over whether it was part of the DMV area, the city tried to characterize itself in any way to stand apart from Baltimore and the nation's capital.

"I don't know why you took the part of the plan about not leaving so literally," Dom said.

"Because I knew you would lose touch," Kendra said. "Sure, you could talk to me, your parents, other friends—but it's different from actually being here. You missed out on a lot, Dom."

"Did I miss out, or did you?" Dom said with more force than expected.

"What's that supposed to mean?"

"You're the one who missed out on getting the education I got, and now you're mad I'm the only one of us who can actually make a real impact here." Dom felt his heart racing.

Water gathered in Kendra's eyes. Shortly before Dom left for California, she told him that she was pursuing a certificate in art and design.

"So, what I'm doing is worthless to you?" Kendra asked, puzzled.

"We agreed to do all we could to support our neighborhood. I went and became a therapist to be able to directly help people," Dom began explaining. "I know you were always talented with art; I just feel like you didn't take a chance on doing something more."

"Are you fucking serious?" Kendra slammed on the brakes. Dom was ready to shoot a response back to her when he realized the question wasn't directed at him. Kendra gripped and pulled on the steering wheel as if she could pull the car back from the object hurtling toward it. A small, four-propellered drone zoomed toward them and skipped off the hood, taking a line of paint with it. It came in so fast it likely would have cracked the windshield had the car not stopped short.

"Where the hell did that come from?" Dom asked. He saw the muscles in Kendra's jaw tensing as she glared past him and over his shoulder.

Two young-looking white guys in black polo shirts came running over from the park, one with a remote control in his hand. "Oh my god! We're so sorry!" the one with the remote said, one hand balling up his blond hair.

"I told you to let me fly it," the other one added.

Kendra was about to open her door to confront the duo, but Dom put his hand on her shoulder, motioning to a police car parked up the street. Kendra leaned partway out her window to look at the scratch and then back at the two guys. "I don't care who was flying that thing. Somebody is paying for the damage, right?"

"For sure," the poorly-skilled pilot said, "we'll let our boss know—" an elbow to the side from his buddy stopped him.

"Here, if you have a cash-sharing app, I'll just send you a stack now," the friend said. Kendra pulled out her phone, allowing the man to scan the QR code on her screen for the transaction. "Sorry again," he said before the two walked away. He pushed the pilot in the back toward where the drone had landed in the street, one of the propellers broken off.

Dom watched the police car for any reaction as Kendra transferred the money to her bank account. "Dude didn't even flinch giving you a thousand dollars. Guess you can fly those things however you want when you're rich."

When the pilot picked up the damaged drone, the reflective bottom surface briefly flashed a logo as the sunlight hit it. Even with the distance, the enlarged capital "A" overlaying a grid-like globe was unmistakable. "Atlasal? I didn't know they made drones now," he said.

Kendra looked back, but the two men had walked out of sight. She looked at Dom with a shrug. "Seems like they make whatever makes money nowadays," she responded. "I'm more worried about why those two dudes were flying that expensive ass drone in our park. Like there's no parks anywhere else in the city."

As they began to roll down the block again toward Dom's house, the driver's side met that of the police car. The officer looked over with the effort of a sleepy dog, and simply shook his head from behind dark shades.

CHAPTER

TWO

THE UNASSUMING BROWN BRICKS AND GREEN AW-
ning hanging over the porch of Dom's childhood home
were a comforting sight after living on a university cam-
pus for two years. The modest, two-story house held the
memories of everything he'd ever known. His door was
already opening before Kendra brought the car to a stop
on the curb in front of the house.

The trip had ended on a tense note, even before
the drone incident, but Kendra looked over with a soft
smile. "Go. Your folks have waited long enough."

Dom hopped out the car, rushing over the concrete walkway and up the steps to the porch. His house
keys were in the duffel bag in the backseat, so he rang
the doorbell and waited, rocking side to side. The door
opened and before Dom could even react, he was in his

mother's tight embrace, hunching down as her arms draped around his neck.

He instantly felt the shaking sobs as his mom gently whispered, "We missed you so much."

"I know," he replied with teary eyes. "I missed you guys, too." Phone and video calls just hadn't been enough.

Dom lifted his head to wipe away his tears and take in his mother's presence. Her face still barely gave a clue as to her age. *"The simple power of moisturizing,"* she would say. She eagerly waved him inside the house as her mood shifted to excitement.

"C'mon, c'mon. Act like you're gonna stay awhile."

"Okay, okay, just let me grab my stuff."

His mom waved at Kendra as she popped the trunk open. She walked in the house while Dom hoisted his luggage out of the car. He placed everything in the corner by the stairs near the front door.

His mom was moving into the kitchen. "Dad will be right down. I'm still getting the 'Hall Family Special' ready for dinner, so you two just make yourselves comfortable like usual."

Dom and Kendra awkwardly entered the living room together, unsure what to say to each other. The room had been rearranged since he was last home, but the warmly colored walls provided the same atmosphere. He scanned the family photos along the walls and tables, taking in the good times spent with his parents. They didn't have much money when he was younger, but had always made the best of the situation. Them not being able to afford to visit him at school or attend his graduation made this reunion that much more special. Just then, Dom heard strong footsteps come down the stairs with the rush of anticipation.

Dom's dad seemed to almost slide into the living room, his long, gray locs trailing behind him. "Freedom!" his dad shouted with his arms raised. "My boy is finally back!"

Dom leaned back with a laugh before wrapping his arms around his dad. A smirk stayed on his face as he thought about all the confusion around his name over the years. Most people assumed his full name was Dominic, not knowing that his dad had a thing for symbolism and had instead chosen to name him Freedom. By first grade, Dom had already decided he needed to go by a nickname to avoid weird looks and teasing, but his dad never missed an opportunity to remind him of the strength behind his name. *"Free them all, Freedom Hall!"* he would say.

His dad loosened his grip around Dom. "Sit, man, sit! How does it feel to be home?" Dom sat on the couch with a cushion between him and Kendra while his dad sat across from them in his blue recliner.

"That coast-to-coast flight is no joke, for sure," Dom said, "but I'm excited to be back in the city."

"Yeah, two years without you hasn't been the same. We're glad you came back," his dad said, a somber tone entering his voice. Dom had worried about making his parents empty nesters. They had done so much to care for whoever entered their home, he figured they could use the break, but he knew it was a risk to leave them alone for so long.

"The time will be worth it. I promise," Dom said. "Once I start this job—"

"Excuse me," Kendra interjected, getting up to pass between Dom and his dad. "I'm going to help out Mrs. Hall while you two talk about the super important work Dom will be doing." She briskly moved toward the kitchen.

Dom rolled his eyes as his dad gave him a puzzled look. "Don't worry about it. We just had a little disagreement in the car."

"Well, I know you two will work it out," his dad said. "You always have."

Dom nodded. "Like I was saying, I'm really excited about the new job. I got pretty good at this therapy thing through my internship. I can't wait to start helping kids in Parkside."

"They sure do need it."

Ding! The timer in the kitchen went off.

His mom announced, "Dom, go put your stuff upstairs and get washed up so we can all eat. And, Abraham, come help set the table up."

His dad silently gave a mock salute in his mom's direction as Dom went to grab his bags.

Dom paused at the bottom of the steps, his heart thumping right up under his suddenly dry throat. He walked up each step like he was on a stair climber machine, pushing down to force his body up to the next one. At the top of the staircase he paused, staring at the closed door to the first bedroom. His parents had begun converting it into an office a couple months before he left for grad school, but had not shown him the finished result, nor had he asked to see it. He cautiously opened the door, pushing through the urge to run from the past hidden behind it.

Inside, a pristine wooden desk sat with a black office chair perfectly centered in front of it. No computer or papers littered the space. The lack of dust was the only hint that someone came in the room to at least keep it clean. The bookshelf on the side of the room where a bed used to be was also spotless. Books were neatly aligned with no obvious system of categorization, inviting onlookers to explore their spines. Sunlight came through the window, pointing Dom to the picture frame resting on the second shelf from the top.

Donned in a graduation cap, the image of Dom's cousin, Maurice, stared back at him. It was as if his eyes could see into the room at that very moment. They reflected the camera flash, but the pin of light was swallowed by the cavern of his expression, one corner of his mouth raised. Dom remembered Senior Picture Day and how hard it was for his mom to convince Maurice to put the cap on and, "Take the best photo you can. It's your day." He had compromised but refused to wear a tie. Despite the clear distress pulling at the seams of

Maurice's attempt at happiness, it was truly the best picture they had left of him.

Dom and Maurice were the type of cousins who spent more than just birthdays, holidays, and family celebrations together. They went to different schools, but were the same age and were each an only child, so their bond became closer to that of siblings. Everything changed, though, when Maurice's mom died.

It was around seventh grade when Dom's mom first told him that Auntie Grace was sick. Some type of lung disease. Even now, his mom hadn't told him much about the illness because she couldn't bear thinking back to losing her sister. It was the beginning of high school when she finally passed and Maurice came to live with them.

Dom remembered learning very quickly that grief was a physical thing. Maurice had played linebacker throughout middle school, but lost his ever-developing athletic build not long after settling into the room Dom was now standing in. It had always been just Maurice and his mom; her loss sapped everything out of him.

Maurice continued to decline throughout high school, somehow scraping by just enough to walk across the stage at graduation. Most of his time outside of school had been spent isolated in his room. There was no forcing him to go to college, so he basically stayed in that room as Dom pursued his degree while still living at home. He and his parents had tried their best to support his cousin until one summer evening after Dom's freshman year, Maurice simply walked out of the house and did not come back. Dom's parents suspected drugs for a while and thought he went out in search of something to use.

Police searched, the story was in the news briefly, but Maurice was never found. No clues, no body, no nothing. Dom remembered the house being full of tears and worries and the neighborhood full of uncertainty. It was hard for Dom to wrap his mind around the series of events that led to his cousin's disappearance five years ago, but it became a formative experience in why he chose to pursue a career in mental health.

Why did Maurice's grief get so bad so fast, and why didn't he see any other options besides running away? What could have helped him? The mystery hung like a thick cloud over Dom's head.

A hand on his shoulder made him turn.

Kendra stood there, a somber look wiping away the remaining tension between them. "The food's ready. Your mom was gonna yell upstairs, but she figured you were in here." She stuffed her hands in her jacket and bit the inside of her lower lip as she looked at the framed picture behind Dom. "I miss him too, man. Y'all were like a package deal. So much was lost that we can't get back." She looked down, realizing her mistake.

Unlike his parents, Dom had never accepted the idea that Maurice was dead and had told Kendra as much. She couldn't imagine what it was like to see the authorities taper down their search so soon and for friends, neighbors, and professors to stop checking in with him about the situation. She didn't know what he did with all the pain inside him.

CHAPTER
THREE

The scent of his mom's cooking met Dom at the bottom of the stairs. He hadn't yet been entrusted with her secret seasoning recipes, probably due to his lack of skill in the kitchen. He and Kendra sat across from each other at the dining room table as his mom set out all the food.

His mom looked at him. "You saw the new room," she said.

Dom gave a quick downward nod. "Thanks for keeping his picture in there." His fork clanked against the plate as he mindlessly pushed food around.

"Why don't you tell Dom about the block party, Kendra," his mom said, changing the subject.

"Oh, it's not that big a deal, Mrs. Hall," Kendra responded.

His dad joined in. "You were just saying the other day that you were glad Dom was coming home in time for the block party. Now it's just some little thing?"

"Um, well," Kendra hesitated. She kept her eyes on her plate. Then, as if she were bored with her own words said, "It's just this thing happening over on Randolph Road next weekend to celebrate the start of summer break for the kids. This art group that I run for high schoolers is going to have an interactive activity set up. You're welcome to come," her eyes met Dom's, "if that's something you're interested in."

A heat seemed to rise from Dom's chest, only able to escape out of his mouth. "Oh, get over it!" His parents froze with their forks in hand. "You're so dramatic about everything. I gave you my opinion in the car and now you're going to keep coming at me with these slick little comments?"

"Really? That was just your opinion? You basically told me that I didn't try hard enough to get on your level. You're so full of yourself you can't even acknowledge how messed up that was." She shoved her chair back. "I'm so sorry, Mr. and Mrs. Hall. I really wanted to stay and celebrate Dom this evening, but this is too much." She got up, gathered her things, and stormed out the front door.

"What the hell was that, Dom?" His dad scowled at him. "You haven't seen her in two years and you just decide to run her out of here. For what?"

Dom shoveled food into his mouth but it was cold and devoid of flavor at that point.

"Do not ignore your father," his mom ordered.

Dom shook his head in frustration. "I'm sorry. It's just a lot being back here. I need to sleep it off." He left the table and went upstairs to his room.

COINS RATTLED AS THE DRESSER REVERBERATED with the vibration of Dom's phone. He had gone to sleep so fed up with Kendra that he forgot the plans he had made for the next morning. Looking at his phone, a series of texts showed that he was going to be late.

Give me thirty and I'll be there, Dom typed.

He shuffled over to his still unpacked suitcase to find clothes to put on. He hoped he would be able to get out of the house without his parents noticing, but he heard their footsteps downstairs as he left his room. The rumbling of his stomach told him he needed to at least try to swipe something small out of the kitchen before heading out.

Nothing was going to be quick and easy based on the looks on their faces when he came across them at the dining table. If not for their change of clothes, he would have thought they'd been waiting for him there since last night.

"And where are you sneaking off to?" his dad asked.

"I'm not sneaking," Dom replied. "I was supposed to meet Nate down at the barbershop a while ago, and don't want to hold him up any longer." He moved around the corner to the fridge to pour himself some orange juice and grabbed a green apple from the basket on the counter.

"Slow down, now," his dad said. "Let's not act like last night didn't happen. You don't have your own place yet. Your mother and I don't need you creating drama in our home."

Dom heard his mom tapping her nails on the table. "More importantly, we know how close you and Kendra are, and that exchange you two had wasn't right," she added as Dom came back to the table with the apple perched in his mouth.

He nonchalantly shrugged while swirling his orange juice like wine. "It's really not a big deal. Friends fight sometimes. It's a sign of a close relationship when you can express emotions, especially the difficult ones, openly."

His mom pursed her lips. "You can hide behind that therapy speak all you want, but I know you both too well. What I saw was you being dismissive. You're grown enough to handle it however you want, though. I just want you to know that you were wrong." His dad nodded in agreement.

Between crunches of his breakfast, Dom thought about what his mom said. As much as he missed Kendra, things had blown up pretty quickly between them on his first day home. He hated how she made it seem like he had done something to her personally by going away to school. He couldn't force her to understand his intentions, though, so why should he keep trying?

"Well, I'm gonna get out of here before Nate ends up mad at me too," he said. "Can't lose two friends in two days."

Outside, Dom looked down at his phone, seeing he still had enough time to walk to the barbershop. It felt like he could finally exhale instead of being squeezed by the pressure of all that took place in the house over the last half day.

He started off on the familiar path he'd taken with his dad countless times to the shop. Although it was the weekend, he didn't see many people out until he got to the intersection where Parkside Library stood. People of all ages came in and out of the front entrance. A couple of kids ran right in front of him and across the crosswalk as they talked excitedly about getting on the library computers early to play games. From across the street, as the kids ran through the open door, Dom was able to make out the sign plastered on it, announcing the Randolph Road Block Party. He let out a sigh, turned, and continued on his way.

When Dom reached the corner a few more blocks down, Nate was already there, leaning against the stop sign. Nate had played football alongside Maurice, but had continued through high school and college. As Dom dapped him up, he was reminded of their difference in strength.

"What's good, bro?" Nate said with a deep voice. "It's been a minute." Nate sounded calm and cool no matter the situation.

"I'm alright. Sorry I'm late. Long flight yesterday, so I wasn't about to be up early," Dom explained.

"Yeah, I feel you, but you know how the shop is on the weekend," Nate responded. "Let's go," he said, pointing his thumb back over his shoulder.

They walked into the packed barbershop, the buzz of clippers and lively conversation filling the space. Every barber had a customer in their chair, and all the seats around the shop were taken. Dom gave a nod to the barbers and shook hands with a couple of the older men he had become familiar with over time.

The two joined the rest of the standing crowd, finding a spot in the corner to wait their turns. "So, what's been up with you? I haven't heard much from you since you went to Cali," Nate said, mockingly throwing up the "west coast" sign with both hands.

Dom chuckled. "Just a lot of studying, man. A little bit of sand and sunshine mixed in, but mostly a lot of work."

"Ay, you're my guy, Dom," Nate began with a smirk, "but you're the only dude I know that could find a way to make living in California sound boring. I always told you you were too smart for your own good."

Something Dom appreciated about his friends from high school and college was that they allowed him to be himself. A little jab here and there was expected, but overall, they respected how dedicated he was academically. "I had to stay focused. Didn't want to waste my time when I knew why I chose to go all the way out there in the first place."

"Mmhmm. Mr. Freedom." Nate squinted his eyes while nodding, pretending to be deep in thought. "Well, your girl Kendra definitely had no idea why you had to go all the way over there. I swear, every time I brought your name up over these past couple years, she would just get all in her feelings."

"Yeah, she picked me up from the airport yesterday, and things didn't go too well," Dom said. A chair opened up, but the other customers were waiting for their preferred barbers. Nate let Dom know that the barber with the empty spot was newer, but did a good job. Dom decided to give him a shot.

"I'm starting a new job, so I need to look sharp," he explained to the barber. "Just take it low."

"Where you gonna be working?" Nate asked.

"This place called New Horizons," Dom answered. "It's not too far from Parkside. Shouldn't be too bad getting there from the house while I'm still looking for my own place."

"Dope," Nate said. "I mean, therapy isn't for me, but these kids now? They need it. You're gonna stay busy." A chair opened up for Nate, and the two spent the rest of the time listening and chiming in to the various conversations and debates going on around them.

CHAPTER

FOUR

Dom leaned forward, keeping his back off the seat and a gap between his shirt and his chest. Between the summer heat and the poor circulation on the bus, his main goal was making it to his first day of work without sweating through his clothes. He thought back to this time of year on the school bus as a kid, when everybody was getting antsy about the end of the school year. The ride to and from school would sound more like a party bus, as all the kids were excitedly anticipating summer plans.

The bus Dom was on now though was full of adults with no break on the horizon. Although Dom worked small jobs here and there in college, the prospect of entering the "real" world and working day in and day out remained a daunting one. His first day at New Horizons was one he had been looking forward to, though. They were just beyond the boundaries of Parkside when the bus came to its first stop since he got on. A woman in a fast-food uniform sitting toward the front got off. From behind him, a few more people trailed off the bus, walking toward a strip mall with only about half of the spaces occupied by a store of some sort.

Next to the strip mall was a familiar older building, its chipped paint and fading sign showing how long it had been since it was active. It was a building Dom's parents would point out what felt like every time they drove by it. It had been a popular nightclub that operated from the time they were in their teens to when they were past their partying days and beginning their journey as parents. As a Black-owned club, it had been a hub of the surrounding community until the strip mall was built next door, bringing with it the complaints of business owners who didn't want a certain type of crowd to frequent their stores and cause trouble. The fact that stores had come and go in that space, and the ones there now likely employed the same type of people previously seen as a nuisance made Dom shake his head as the bus continued on its route.

When the bus came to his stop, Dom was already standing at the front, with his black messenger bag flung over his shoulder. He began the short walk to work with brisk steps, ensuring he wasn't late on his first day. Finally, he was going to begin fulfilling his calling.

As he rounded the corner to the street New Horizons was on, a clamor of metal rang out beneath him. Looking down, he realized he had accidentally kicked over a plastic cup full of coins, dispersing them out in different directions. A homeless man sitting up against the corner building opened his eyes and shifted slowly.

"I'm so sorry, sir. I'll pick them all up for you," Dom said as he scrambled around the sidewalk. Several people passed by, none stopping to help. No one even gave Dom a judgmental look; they simply walked by as if they didn't see anything.

"I wasn't watching where I was going. I'm so sorry."

Once he gathered the coins back into the cup, he reached into his pocket and added a ten-dollar bill, putting the cup closer to the mass of coats and blankets surrounding the man. The man looked up at Dom briefly, scratching at his dust-sprinkled afro before wrapping himself up tighter and going back to sleep. A feeling of guilt held onto Dom's stomach as he continued down the street.

He finally arrived at a building with midnight blue paneling on the front, its roof reaching one story above its neighbors on either side. He approached glass doors with the words *New Horizons Health Center* printed across them. They slid open with barely a sound. Pushing through a second set of doors, he froze when he entered the lobby. He had interviewed for the job over a video call while still in California, and their website didn't have any images of the inside of the center. Seeing it now, he doubted whether photos could do it justice.

Smooth white walls surrounded the space. Keeping it from a bland hospital feel, light blue lights shone up from the baseboards, giving the room a soft, inviting glow. A few empty chairs lined either side of the room. The only person present was a blonde woman sitting at the desk in front of him, head down in her tablet. The room was so pristine, he felt like he needed to tiptoe his way up to her.

"Name, please?" she asked, looking up from the tablet.

Dom was taken in by the large screen behind her, displaying the New Horizons logo against a moving backdrop of softly flowing ocean water.

"Name?" the woman asked again.

"Hi, uh. Dom. Dom Hall," he answered.

"Oh! One of our new employees, right?" She introduced herself as Elane, as she skittered around the desk, scrolling through her tablet again. "Follow me this way, please."

Dom followed her around the wall with the big screen and through a previously unseen door.

"We have some other new staff starting today," she explained. "You all will be going through our orientation training shortly, but first I'm going to have you meet with your supervisor so you two can start getting acquainted."

They came to a stairwell and walked up to the second floor. "All the supervisors' offices are up here. Your supervisor, Amalia, will let you know where your office will be down on the first."

"And up there?" Dom looked up the stairwell to the third floor.

"That's the CEO's office. She's out of town, but I'd still get in trouble if I gave you a tour of her space." Elane opened the second-floor stairwell door. "Amalia is right here in this first office. Stop by the front desk anytime if you need anything!" She smiled, checked something off on her tablet, and went back downstairs.

Dom took a deep breath before knocking on the slightly ajar door.

"Come in," a voice said from inside.

A strong smell of lavender was the first thing that greeted him. A scent diffuser was hard at work on a small table in the corner of the office. "You must be Dom. I'm Amalia Baker, and I'll be your clinical supervisor." She stood to shake his hand.

Confidence beamed from her vibrant smile and proudly displayed curly afro. Her dark skin was complemented by purple feather earrings and a purple blazer that rested over a t-shirt and dress pants.

"Nice to meet you. I'm excited to be here," Dom said, sounding almost out of breath as his nerves took over. Sitting in the chair in front of Amalia's desk, he took in one wall that had a bookcase full of psychology textbooks, biographies of famous thinkers in the field, and manuals for different treatment models. The windowsill behind her was spotted with various plants, one of which had a small flag sticking out of its pot that read *All Are Welcome.*

"We're glad to have you at New Horizons!" Amalia said, excitedly clapping. "There's so much cool stuff happening here, I know you're going to love it. You'll get the official spiel in a little bit though, so I'll save all the company buzzwords. Tell me about yourself. What should I know about Mr. Dom?"

Her warm demeanor was a welcome surprise. He was nervous about being a beginner therapist and having his skills critiqued by someone more experienced. He hoped her personality extended to her work style. "I don't know what you want to know, but I guess the most important thing to me is that I was born and raised in Selton City. It's important for me to be able to bring that into my work with clients. Let them know that I understand where they come from."

"Amazing!" Amalia said. "I only moved here a few years ago, so I'm always happy to know that people from the community will be serving those from their community. And, you know…" she rubbed the back of her hand with a finger, "that's just the cherry on top." She gave a knowing downward nod. "Don't worry, I'll have your back. I know how hard it is for us."

In grad school, Dom was made to feel like a unicorn. Being a Black male therapist, people seemed to cherish his basic existence while expecting so much out of him that it felt like he had to put on a performance. Although his goal was to help people in his community, he wanted to do it on his own terms. If Amalia could understand that, they would get along fine.

They chatted a little bit more. She told him about her clinical experiences and specialization in trauma in Black girls. He shared more about growing up in Parkside and how much the people he grew up around shaped him.

Amalia looked down at her watch. "Let's head over to the conference room. There's a special presentation for all staff before the new employee orientation, so everybody's waiting."

The conference room was dominated by a large, horseshoe shaped table. The chairs lining it were already filled, leaving a handful of people standing in the back. Dom found a spot to stand, leaning against a wall. A tall guy in a blue and white checkered shirt squinted through his thick-rimmed glasses as he approached.

"Oh, I see they hired another one of us. What's better than one token? Two," he said with a toothy smile. "I'm just playing. I'm Louis."

"Dom. Nice to meet you." He noticed the pen perched on Louis' ear with the Selton Cyclones logo, the city's pro-basketball team, on it. "Wow, you gotta be from here to be brave enough to rep them. We've *been* trash."

Louis laughed. "Yeah, I grew up a little ways from here uptown. Gotta support 'em even when it hurts. You from here too?"

"Parkside."

"Oh, you're *really* from here. New Horizons must be glad they found you. Credibility and all." Louis looked around the room. "It's really just your supervisor over there and us. There's been some other Black people here before but turnover is rough. All of us working for the same white woman though. Stacy Connors, CEO of New Horizons." He said her name and title with a flourish of his hands like the words were surrounded by lights.

"I get it, but at least they're trying to reflect the people in the area with the staff, right?" Dom offered.

"Ha!" Louis crossed his arms. "I've been here a few years, and let me tell you, NH doesn't do anything past the bare minimum to serve its clients."

"You're still here though. Why?"

Louis shrugged. "Sadly, it's better than places I worked before. I provide therapy to the best of my abilities, but that doesn't make up for a company that cares more about its bottom line than the well-being of the people it serves." Two claps interrupted their exchange.

Amalia stood in the center of the horseshoe. "Alright everybody! Our admin team is running a little behind, but I've been given the green light to go ahead and start the presentation." A small slot opened in the ceiling above her and a wide screen slid down. The lights dimmed, bringing a hush to the room as a projected video began to play.

A red-haired, freckled woman smiled on the screen. *"Hi, I'm Stacy Connors, CEO of New Horizons."*

Louis looked over at Dom out of the corner of his eye, mouth twisted with a see-what-I-mean expression.

"Thank you for choosing to be a part of our team. Get ready to see what's beyond the horizon..." her voice faded out as the camera quickly panned across an ocean and then flashed to a montage of scenes depicting people in the midst of various activities: a man dressed for work getting into his car, a child landing smoothly at the bottom of a slide, women gathered in a circle laughing; all the people in the montage looked content and at ease. Dom noticed that most of them were Black and recognized the setting of the video as Selton City.

"Here at New Horizons, we know that people encounter obstacles to accomplishing what they want in life." Images of tearful faces...yellow police tape...empty alcohol bottles...a bruised face. The word TRAUMA blinking in and out on the screen. *"We also recognize that there is not equal access to the resources that can help people best overcome their struggles."* A white couple sitting across from a therapist in a carefully decorated office. A young woman receiving a prescription discretely delivered to her door. *"That's why we've decided to bring a highly innovative and proven treatment option right to those who will benefit from it the most."*

Another white woman, with shoulder-length, jet-black hair and icy blue eyes, appeared on the screen. People shifted in their seats, leaning forward. A man standing a few feet in front of Dom let out a loud whispered, "What?" The person in the video was someone anybody not living under a rock knew.

"Hello, I'm Miranda Webb, founder and CEO of Atlasal." Dom took his back off the wall, tilting his head as he listened more closely. *"I'm so happy to be able to talk to you about the new collaboration we have with New Horizons."* A short huff came from Louis.

Stacy came back on the screen as the camera pulled back, showing the two women sitting together in a nicely decorated room. She continued, *"Since New Horizons opened, we have been intentional in using the latest trauma-informed principles to guide the therapeutic modalities we offer to our clients. But over my more than twenty years in various roles throughout the health sector, I've learned about one of the industry's dirtiest little secrets. The most innovative treatments that push mental health care forward are rarely made accessible to the people who need them most. The pipeline from research to utilization to access is consistently clogged by bureaucracy, funding incentives, and outright bias. Our friends at Atlasal have decided to change that."*

Miranda took over. She had become known over the years for her comfortable charisma, delivering tech conference presentations, graduation speeches, and online livestreams with the same engaging demeanor. *"At*

Atlasal, we truly believe that the best doesn't have to wait. As we have expanded our product offerings over the past few years, we realized the importance of bridging the gaps to bring the highest quality mental health services to communities that are too often forgotten about. And with that, I'd like to introduce you to Atlasal's virtual reality mental health care program, Haven."

A sleek, white headset appeared, a holographic Atlasal logo flashing on its side. The company had started off as a maker of home appliances. Their expansion into other electronics like headphones and tablets began after Miranda Webb was named as the new leader almost a decade ago. Her daring moves helped her to rapidly obtain billionaire status. Apparently, drones were another recent expansion, but this step into virtual reality and mental health care was a real surprise. Dom was somewhat aware of the advances in using VR to treat certain mental health conditions, but didn't think he would be utilizing it so early in his career.

"I am personally so proud of what our team has developed with Haven," Miranda continued. *"With this program, people suffering from a range of mental health disorders will be able to explore a world of all new possibilities. Haven is a home. It is a place where people can try new things, learn more about themselves, and create a version of themselves they've only imagined. And no, I'm not just referring to a digital avatar. Through the various functions of Haven, users will be able to apply the skills they build to their real lives, transforming them for*

the better. You all will be the first wave of clinicians integrating Haven into New Horizons' therapeutic offerings. We can't wait to see the results."

Stacy, beaming with pride, closed out. *"Welcome to this new journey we are on and thank you again for choosing to be a part of our team."*

As the lights came back on, everyone looked around at each other. Heads nodded, a couple smiles were exchanged, and one pair excitedly rattled off questions to each other. Louis seemed to be the only one not impressed. "Quite the infomercial. Miranda Webb sure knows how to sell something."

Dom wondered how recently the partnership with Atlasal had been formed. It seemed it would be a pretty strong recruitment tool, but it wasn't mentioned in his interview. "You don't think the clients coming to New Horizons deserve access to the latest technology? You just said they don't do enough to really help people."

"Look, my Black ass is not about to rock the boat over it," Louis said. "I'm just saying that Atlasal didn't make this deal because they're going to *lose* money. Shit, it probably works both ways. Now that I think about it, I bet this deal is how NH was able to renovate the front lobby. Business is business, I guess."

Amalia stepped back into the center of the table. "I know that was a surprise to everyone. Pretty amazing, right? I've seen the headsets myself, and I'm so ready for you all to start using them. Please, go enjoy your lunch break, and then you'll be meeting one of the programmers from Atlasal who's going to give you some initial training on Haven."

CHAPTER

FIVE

Excited chatter filled the conference room post-lunch, much of the staff still riding high from the announcement. Conversations cut off quickly once a man entered sporting a navy-blue t-shirt with a white Atlasal logo across his chest. He held a box under one arm, dragging a stool in with the other. "Hey, everyone, I'm David, one of the Senior Programmers with Atlasal. My partner, Kyle, was supposed to help with the demo today, but he had to finish up with another project last minute." He spoke in a way that sounded like he was annoyed to be there. "I know Haven pretty well though, since I helped design it, so we should be good."

Dom's focus wavered as he suddenly recognized David. He was the guy who paid Kendra for the drone accident. He had a feeling Kyle was the pilot. So, they were able to be reckless with the drone because they worked for the multi-billion-dollar corporation that made it. Dom didn't think David had seen his face in Kendra's car, but he still felt uneasy.

"I'm going to give you all an overview of the program today, and then you'll have plenty of time to get some practice in the rest of the week," David said. "The headset is pretty standard," he continued, pulling the device out of the box and placing it on the stool. Like he said, it didn't look much different from other VR headsets. Kind of like heavier, clunkier snow goggles, Dom had always thought. "It's sturdier than other models on the market, but the real magic is in the software," David explained.

The screen lowered from the ceiling again, with a slideshow now displayed. In bold, all-caps, white letters, the word *HAVEN* hung over an open field in a clear, blue sky. "So, the first thing I want to make sure you all know," David began, "is that Haven is not meant to replace therapists. In fact, it's designed to incorporate you all into its programming. Truly, without you all, Haven wouldn't function." He moved the slideshow along through a series of diagrams as he explained further. "The treatment protocol begins with standard therapy sessions. You guys do your thing, and all Haven does is listen. After three sessions, Haven's proprietary algorithm will have gathered enough information to know what type of virtual environment will be best for the client. It will then use the recordings to re-produce your voice—vocabulary, cadence, and all—to be a guide in the VR sessions."

Louis' hand shot up. "Wait, wait, wait. I don't even use the voice commands for my TV remote. You want us to let a computer program copy our voices so it can say things we could just say ourselves? What does Atlasal do with our conveniently captured voices?"

"Understandable concerns." David's reply sounded like a script. "First, the point of recreating the therapist's voice is to maintain the client's level of immersion in the VR environment. Although the therapist will be able to see what the client is seeing on another screen, an external audio input would distract the client from their treatment. And as far as voice data, Atlasal and New Horizons already have it in the contract that none of it can be used outside of the described primary function. Our cybersecurity team is top-notch as well."

Dom looked over at Louis; he didn't appear any less skeptical. "All that information will be in the client consent forms, right?" Dom asked. He suddenly felt nervous as David's eyes shifted to him.

David averted his gaze over to Amalia at the side of the room, brow raised.

"Yes, of course," she answered. "We'll be doing another training in the next few days to get you all confident with explaining the system to clients."

David continued. "Following the initial three-session configuration stage, the client will then interact with the VR environment for the first half of each subsequent session, while the therapist works to integrate the experience to close out the session. The environments incorporate lots of nature-based elements, providing enhanced relaxation and potential for emotional exploration. I personally think it also offers a great contrast to the urban environment here." The way he used the word "urban" sludged through Dom's ears.

"The other advantage of our program is in its utilization of data." David switched to a slide full of charts and graphs. "Haven is constantly collecting data to keep track of your client's progress. This measurement-based approach takes out the guess work of typical therapy, allowing you and your client to know exactly how well the treatment is working. With easy access to the data readouts, you'll both be on the same page throughout the duration of care."

A helpful feature, Dom thought. He wanted to be precise in the care he provided. In grad school, he'd learned all about various assessments and questionnaires used to track clients' symptoms. He and his classmates used a couple pretty rudimentary ones in their internship experiences, but he found out that most of his professors with private practices didn't bother with rigorous measurement. They felt that over-quantification changed the process of therapy too much.

"Which leads me to a special announcement," David said, pulling his phone from his pocket. "Let me make sure I get this right." He tapped and scrolled a bit before clearing his throat to read. "Atlasal is extremely excited to work with New Horizons on delivering the highest quality care to those most in need. Your hard work is what will make this opportunity flourish. Given the effort involved, we figured a special gift was in store. Whichever New Horizons therapist has the biggest measured symptom improvement for their client caseload will receive a bonus and get to have a one-on-one meeting with CEO, Miranda Webb, when she comes to visit Selton City in September."

Everyone beamed and began clapping except for Louis, although he looked intrigued. "I'm all for extra money," he said to Dom. "I don't know what I'd talk to Miranda about though."

"Anything, I'd imagine," Dom said. "All the people she knows, all the resources she has. Sounds like a once in a lifetime opportunity."

"You really think she would help one of us into her billionaire circles? I'd rather get free Atlasal products for life, thank you very much."

Dom shook his head at Louis' cynicism, hoping he wasn't like this about everything. David wrapped his presentation, opening up the floor for questions. People's questions were more focused on Miranda Webb's visit and the bonus than about Haven.

Amalia shrugged when asked about the bonus amount; it seemed the announcement was a surprise to her, too. Miranda's appearance was only three months away, so although he liked the idea of data-driven care, Dom wondered how any of them would become proficient enough with the Haven program to see any meaningful results by then. They wouldn't even start using it with clients until next week following further training with the software. He hoped the days would fly by so he could dive into client work, but remembered the block party was on Saturday.

He owed Kendra a visit.

CHAPTER

SIX

DOM LAID IN BED, THE SUN SHINING THROUGH HIS curtains keeping him from drifting back into what had been a fitful sleep. This wasn't the day to sleep in anyway. He dragged himself out of bed and downstairs, greeted by his already fully dressed and ready to go parents.

"You know the block party starts in an hour, right?" his dad asked.

"Yes, and I know I don't need to be there right when it starts," Dom said as he rubbed his eyes. "I'm not in a rush."

"Well, we're just trying to get there to enjoy everything before it gets unbearably hot," his mom said.

"I still need some time to get ready, so don't worry. You guys can leave without me. I'll catch a bus with Nate and meet you there." The exchange with his parents made him regret even more not locking down an apartment before returning from school. He'd gotten used to moving at his own pace.

Nate and Dom hopped on the bus heading toward Randolph Road. The street was an important one to the community. It demarcated Parkside from adjacent neighborhoods and was dubbed with the last name of Selton's only mayor to have ever been born and raised in Parkside. Mayor Julius Randolph's reputation stood strong over the past nearly half-century since he was in office; his focus on serving the needs of all the people in the city had earned him the nickname, "Mayor of the Masses".

The bus was packed. "You think everyone's going to the block party?" Nate asked. Dom texted Kendra the night before, hoping she'd had time to cool off and to see if she knew how many people were expected to show up, but he got no answer.

"I don't know. It's a new event, but it's hard to pass up on food, music, and arts and crafts for the kids," Dom answered.

"I remember when we'd be on the bus as kids when it was this packed," Nate said. "Me and Maurice had that little 'bad kid' streak where we competed to see who could take the most expensive thing out of someone's bag. Terrible, right?"

"Yeah…" Dom looked down at his feet.

Nate put a hand on his shoulder. "My bad, bro." Dom nodded slightly, letting the silence hang between them. "How's the new job?"

"It's cool." The words drooled out of Dom, suddenly uninterested in what was going on around him.

At the next stop, a girl got on and made her way toward them. It was Britney, one of their high school and college friends. "Hey, what's up y'all? It's been a minute," she said. "Especially you, Dom."

"Good to see you, Britney," Dom replied. Despite the years of school together, he didn't really know her that well on a personal level.

"You going to the block party, too?" Nate asked.

"Yeah, I was supposed to be there early to help Kendra set up, but I slept through my alarm," Britney explained. "She's probably pissed. But not as much as she is at you apparently," she said looking at Dom. "What'd you do? I asked about you the other day and she nearly took my head off."

Dom shrugged. "Don't worry about it. I'm gonna talk to her."

"Okay, whatever." She rolled her eyes and tapped one of her ear buds, turning away from them.

A few minutes later, the bus stopped at the west end of Randolph Road. A large chunk of the passengers got off, all heading toward the balloons and signs attached to the light posts at the entrance to the block party. Britney sped off ahead. Dom thought about following her to wherever Kendra was, but he was struck by everything in front of him.

The street was alive. Loud rhythms bounced and rattled through the asphalt, guiding the movements of kids making dance videos. Charcoal and barbecue punctuated the not-quite-noon air, preparing appetites for an all-day feast. Bean bag tosses, foot races, and an assortment of other activities filled the street with a dynamic energy.

As Dom and Nate began walking through the crowd, Dom felt something return to him. It was like the ground under him had become solid again. He was seeing his home back in action. Two years away had created more of a separation than he'd anticipated. His best friend felt like he'd become a ghost, but the gathering around him right now told him that he was back where he belonged.

"It's dope that Kendra and her people were able to put this together for the kids," Nate said. Dom knew the kids needed it. The light of the joy-filled event cast momentary shadows over the issues they had to deal with every day. Summer was a tough time for him to start practicing therapy. The down time mixed with heat and tension often gave the season more burdens than opportunities to celebrate, so he had an unfortunate hunch that he'd be busy.

They came across Dom's parents at a lemonade stand operated by two young girls. His parents looked tired, having already walked the length of the block party one way and had stopped to rest. It had been a while since Nate last saw them, so he stayed behind to catch up while Dom went looking for Kendra.

He meandered along Randolph Road until he noticed a long line of kids, winding like a rope with a few knots of huddled onlookers in it. He looked ahead until he spotted what they were waiting for. There at the front of the line were Kendra and a few teenagers. One by one, they were giving the kids gloves and socks, each dipped in different colored paint, while Britney stood in the middle of a large canvas, supervising the kids as they decorated it. The giggles and squeals punctuated the kids' movements across the canvas.

Dom walked past the line up to Kendra. She glanced over at him quickly, continuing to give the kids supplies. "Here you go, guys. Make whatever you want out there. Just have fun! And try not to get the paint all over each other!" She kept her back to him.

"Hey, Kendra," Dom said.

"How many gloves do we have left?" Kendra asked one of the teens helping her.

"This is a really cool idea. I would have loved this as a kid," Dom said to her back.

She finally acknowledged him. "It's not just for kids. Art is for all ages," she said over her shoulder with a sarcastic smile. "But thanks. I'm sure you'd be surprised to know the amount of planning it took to put this together."

Dom sighed. "Look, I know you're busy, but I just wanted to talk real quick. I know we left things off on the wrong foot."

Kendra turned toward him, placing a hand on her hip. "Is that how you describe it? Tuh." She went right back to handing out supplies.

Dom wasn't going to leave without them having a real talk. "I ran into one of the guys with that drone again."

Kendra turned back around with raised eyebrows. "Ran into, like, with a car or what? That's about the only thing that would keep them out of our neighborhood." Dom told her about his first day at work and the surprise partnership with Atlasal. He left out the part about the competition to meet Miranda Webb, assuming Kendra wouldn't be thrilled about it.

"So, they were just on a little lunch break when they scratched up my car, huh? I'm still waiting on the shop to finish fixing it." She stepped away from the canvas.

Dom shrugged. "Our initial training with the Haven system is done now, so hopefully David's gone back to wherever he's from and there won't be any more fly-bys."

"You like this job so far? That VR stuff sounds sketchy," Kendra said.

Dom laughed. "You sound like my co-worker, Louis. He's been at New Horizons for a minute and isn't too hyped about having to use VR. I see it as a tool to improve the work I'll be able to do with these kids."

He looked out at the swirling arms and stomping feet ambling across the canvas. "Having the latest tech at my disposal can only help with how much healing is needed here."

"There you go," Kendra said. "The man with the plan. Well, you let me know how that works out." She turned to go back to the canvas.

"Really? What's up with you?"

She faced him again. "I'm just tired of you sounding like you're the prodigal son returning to graciously offer everyone your gifts."

"I don't know why you think—" a scream from several feet away cut him off. A group of kids had scattered, with one on the ground nursing a scraped knee. Others were pointing all in the same direction. Dom followed their fingers to an uncanny site. An e-scooter was gliding across the street toward a row of vendor booths stocked with various products. No one was moving, as they all seemed to be mesmerized by the fact that the scooter had no rider. It was moving with perfect balance, even veering between a few cones in the street as it now appeared to be gaining speed.

Dom jumped into action, pushing past a couple bystanders to catch up to the scooter before it ran into the booths. He grabbed one of the handlebars and pulled it down to the ground a few feet from the vendors. The wheels continued spinning rapidly as the scooter lay on its side.

"You okay, Dom?" Kendra placed a hand on his back as he caught his breath.

"Yeah. I've never seen anything like that."

Two girls came over from the canvas line. "We were all just standing there and then we saw the scooter come shooting out of the alley over there," one said, pointing back to the space between a convenience store and a flower shop.

"Yeah, it hit Andrea's ankle and knocked her over," the other added.

Dom and Kendra looked at each other. He looked at the handlebars, feeling around to see if they had somehow been locked in position to accelerate the scooter. They seemed normal, but even modifying them couldn't explain the scooter turning on its own. Dom stepped over it to check out the underside and see if there was a way to disconnect the battery to stop the wheels. He paused when he saw what was there. An Atlasal logo on the bottom of the deck. He called Kendra over to see it.

"What in the... Are those guys out here again?" She looked around. "You're the one working with them now. This doesn't feel right."

"I don't know what's going on," he said. E-scooters were another product he wasn't aware that Atlasal made. Maybe it was some sort of prototype, but there was no David, Kyle, or anyone else in sight. The rogue scooter groaned as the wheels finally slowed to a stop. The crowd who witnessed everything still seemed a little spooked. A middle-aged man stood up from crouching behind his vendor booth. He walked around it to pick the scooter up by the handlebars, dragging it off the street while muttering about all this tech craziness.

CHAPTER

SEVEN

DOM TOOK CAUTION WHEN HE RETURNED TO work, hesitating along his walk at each street corner and peering down alleys, wary another scooter, drone, or other out of control gadget would cross his path. The weird and unsettling scene from the block party played over again in his head. Who could he tell about it? Word about the incident had spread a bit around the neighborhood over the weekend, but no one was making note of the scooter being an Atlasal product. It probably wasn't relevant. Right? Dom thought about telling Amalia, but if she told David and David wanted to talk to him, would he have to bring up the drone, too? By the time he sat down in the office he'd been assigned last week, he had decided against it. There was too much to focus on with meeting his first client today.

Louis bumped Dom's door open with his shoulder. "You ready for today? I'm on your ass for this contest."

"I thought meeting Miranda wasn't a big deal to you?"

"Doesn't mean I'm not competitive." Louis mimed putting on a headset. "Real world or virtual world, I don't miss a chance to win."

"You're too much, man," Dom chuckled. The notion of competing around improving clients' mental health certainly had its absurdities. Each client was different, so how could their therapy outcomes be compared? Could a therapist really push a client to improve faster than another? Should they?

After Louis left, Dom pulled out the tablet provided by Atlasal to review the client summary for his first session one more time before talking it over with Amalia.

Name: Jasmine Henry Age: 13	NOTES
Symptom(s): sleeplessness, panic attacks, self-isolation	Should assess for anxiety disorder and PTSD.
Presenting Problem: About two months ago, there was a school lockdown due to the building being hit by a stray bullet. Jasmine was traumatized by this and began to miss days of school. Her grades dropped as well, but she was still able to finish on par with her class average. With the school year over, she is afraid about returning next year.	Jasmine's mother, Ms. Henry, shared that the shooter was never identified.
Goal(s): Jasmine's stated goal is to not feel scared anymore. Ms. Henry's stated goal is for Jasmine to be able to return and stay in school and be with her friends.	Ms. Henry and Jasmine seem to have a positive relationship which will assist with goal attainment.

As he arrived at Amalia's office, Dom heard a grainy voice coming through her door. "...this is a reflection of you, too. If the people you're supervising don't know what they're doing, then I can assume the same about you. Put all the fluffy sociocultural stuff aside and focus on the numbers and everything should be fine."

Dom knocked.

"Come on in!" Amalia closed her laptop as Dom entered. "Today's the big day. Are you ready?" she asked as she rubbed the purple amulet on her necklace between her fingers. Her bright tone of voice didn't match the stress in her eyes.

"I'm a little nervous," he said. "This is my first client out in the 'real' world. And it's my first time using Haven so, yeah; nervous."

"Remember, the first three sessions you're just using Haven to record. You do your thing while it does its. Now, let's run through the info from the intake clinician one more time before Jasmine arrives. What stood out the most to you?"

"The trauma, for sure," Dom said. They only had to practice lockdown drills when he was in school. Sounds of late-night gunshots were occasional when he was growing up, but a shootout in the middle of the day and near a school was hard to fathom. He could only imagine how kids like Jasmine felt just stepping outside for recess. How could anyone expect to learn in that environment?

"Yes," Amalia nodded. "Getting back her overall sense of security will start with the safety Jasmine experiences in the therapeutic relationship with you. Trust and connection are your main goals for these early sessions."

A message popped up on Dom's tablet, letting him know Jasmine and her mom had arrived. "Thanks, Amalia. I'll let you know how the session goes."

Before meeting the family, Dom went back to his office to set up Haven. He ran the instructions David gave them through his head. First, he placed the headset on top of an end table, positioning it to create a triangle with the two chairs in the office. This was to ensure the best acoustics for the headset's built-in microphones to capture his and Jasmine's words. With the touch of a button, a small blue light began flashing in the center of the device's eyepiece to indicate it was ready for data collection.

Dom met Ms. Henry and Jasmine in the waiting area. Ms. Henry stood to shake his hand while Jasmine stayed lying on a bean bag chair, twisting the ends of her two long braids together.

"Stand up, Jasmine," Ms. Henry said. "Be polite and say hello to your therapist, Mr. Dominic."

"Oh, just Dom is fine."

Jasmine let out a sigh before getting up. "Hi," the greeting fell from her mouth.

Dom led them back to his office, explaining the Haven setup before starting the session. Both had signed the consent form to allow the system to be utilized, but he wanted to make sure he could answer any of their questions. Ms. Henry said she was okay with whatever would help Jasmine get better.

"It's got games?" Jasmine asked, a slight peak in her voice.

"Sorry, it's not one of those headsets," Dom said. "And it will only be listening to us today." Jasmine's face reflected how weird that sentence sounded. "You'll get to use the VR in a few weeks; I promise." Ms. Henry gave Jasmine a hug before going back to the waiting area.

Dom pushed the button on the side of the headset again, turning the blue light solid. Jasmine slouched in her chair, staring at the device.

"So, do you know why you're here today? Did your mom explain it to you?" Dom asked.

Jasmine glanced at him. "Yeah," she muttered before returning her gaze to the headset.

"What did she tell you?"

"She wants me to keep going to school next year. I hate that place though, so I'm not going back."

"What happened that made you not want to go back?"

Jasmine's leg started bouncing.

Stupid question. You know what happened. You're getting ahead of yourself, Dom thought. *Just focus on the therapeutic relationship. Make her feel safe. Get to know her.*

"We can wait to talk about that," he said. "Do you have anything you want to talk about today?"

"How long do I have to keep coming here?" Jasmine asked.

"Well, I don't know exactly, but how about we see how today goes first? Why don't you tell me about what you have planned for the summer."

Jasmine talked about summer camp and wanting to spend time at her grandma's house. Dom prompted her for more details. She talked about hanging with her half-brother and cousins at her grandma's and the games they liked to play together. In particular, she enjoyed any opportunity to prove she was faster than all the boys in the house. Dom noticed that as she talked about her family more, she sat up in her chair.

"It seems like you have a good time when you're with your family," Dom said.

"Mmhmm."

"Well, I know this place probably isn't like your grandma's house," Dom said looking around the office, "but I want you to feel as comfortable being yourself here as you do when you're with your family."

"Okay..." she muttered.

"What about you and your mom? How do you get along with each other?"

"Good. We don't fight or anything."

Dom was pleased that he was getting Jasmine to talk more, although gaining her trust was going to take more time. Not too many kids beg to be in therapy, so getting them engaged took creativity and patience. The session continued with small talk about Jasmine's interests. One of the most difficult parts of therapy for Dom so far was feeling like he wasn't "doing" anything. Throughout his training in grad school, he would have moments where he questioned any therapeutic techniques that didn't directly address the client's presenting problem. He felt ineffective when he couldn't see the outcome of his work.

After a while, Jasmine's eyelids started to get heavy. Dom took the cue and began wrapping up the session. "I really appreciate you being willing to talk with me today," he said. "I'm going to check-in with your mom briefly before you guys head out, okay?" Jasmine popped out of her seat with newfound energy and scooted out the door. Dom hit the button on the headset one more time before following her out.

Ms. Henry came back to his office. "I'm surprised she talked with you for a whole hour," she said.

"It took some time to get words out of her, but as she gets more comfortable, I'm sure she'll open up."

"Yeah, well, she needs to speed that up. I know summer feels like forever for kids, but when school's back in a few months she needs to be ready. If she starts missing days from the beginning, catching up is only going to get harder."

"What's important at this stage is that Jasmine has your support. She already feels like she doesn't want to be here, so if she gets any more pressure to get better faster, she'll only resist more."

Ms. Henry looked unimpressed. "I'll make sure she knows she has to talk more when we come back next week."

As he watched the Henrys leave the building, he felt a tension leave his shoulders. His first session as a real therapist was done.

THE GLASS BOTTLE SLID THROUGH THE PUDDLE OF condensation. Dom caught it, thanking Louis for buying the first round. Sink Hole was one of several bars that opened in Selton City while he was in grad school. Louis claimed they had one of the best happy hour deals in the city, convincing Dom to unwind a bit after their first day working with clients.

"To New Horizons," Louis said, lifting his beer to the forced pun. Dom followed suit.

"So, how'd your first session go?" Dom asked.

Louis sighed. "All that money Atlasal put into Haven and it decides to malfunction the first time I try to use it. Go figure."

"Really?"

"Yeah, I hit the button to record and got some 'cannot detect' error or something. Oh, and then I found out the client I'm supposed to see tomorrow declined to consent to use Haven! He's an older guy, so probably not into the tech stuff. This damn contest is slipping away from me already."

"It's the client's right to choose, though. More important than the contest, don't you think?"

"I'm still tryna win, but of course I understand the ethics," Louis said with a huff. "My supervisor already drilled it into my head. The most I can do is re-introduce the idea of Haven after I've built some trust in a couple sessions, try to explain it in more detail, and hope he comes around to it."

Dom took a swig of his beer. "Speaking of supervisors, I overheard Amalia having a conversation with someone. Well, it was more like she was getting grilled. Something about focusing more on the numbers."

Louis shrugged. "I'm sure this Atlasal stuff's got everyone under pressure." He got up from his barstool to use the bathroom.

Dom mindlessly scrolled through social media until he came across a post by Kendra. The image showed a house, painted in a child's simple style of a square with a triangular roof. The caption advertised Kendra's first gallery show, entitled H.O.M.E., happening in a couple weeks. Dom liked the post and sent her a text:

Your first gallery show? Dope! I know you're gonna kill it.

He was being genuine and hoped the support could be an olive branch of sorts. The text immediately showed a read notification, but by the time he and Louis left the bar, no response had come.

CHAPTER

EIGHT

"My daughter needs help now!"

The raised voice echoed from the lobby. It wasn't the kind of energy Dom wanted to start his Friday morning with. When he pushed the door open to the lobby, a frenzy was in full swing.

Elane, paler than usual, had her cell phone perched next to her ear. "Ma'am, if you don't lower your voice and give me back my tablet, I'm calling the police!"

Dom tensed. Protocol seemed to have gone out the window. All New Horizons staff knew that calling the police was the last resort if de-escalating a client wasn't working and a mobile crisis team couldn't arrive quickly enough.

"Oh, really? The cops know my daughter's situation, so I'm sure they'd back me up in making sure she gets help." Ms. Henry raised Elane's tablet in one hand, slamming its rubber casing against the desk, emphasizing each word as she repeated, "She! Needs! Help!" over and over. In her other hand was a knot of Jasmine's hoodie. Like a dog on a tight leash, there was nowhere Jasmine could go. Arms crossed and face heavy, she looked more bored than bothered by her current position.

"For the last time, ma'am, we don't do walk-ins," Elane said. "You can take your daughter to the hospital or just wait until her next appointment on Monday with—"

"Me," Dom interrupted. Ms. Henry turned, her laser beam stare redirecting to a new target. "Hey, Ms. Henry." He cleared his throat to remove the shakiness from his voice. "It sounds like something serious is going on, so let's go talk in my office."

"Mr. Dom," Ms. Henry said with a huff, "you're gonna have to do more than talk to this girl." If possible, she would have lifted Jasmine off the ground the way she yanked at her hood. "Big Ms. Jasmine here was missing for the last forty-eight hours, thinking she could just do whatever she wants. Police looking for her and everything." Hurt hovered in the depths of her voice. "She's lucky I brought her here instead of letting the police keep her."

Forty-eight hours in, Dom and his parents had hoped Maurice might still come home. They spoke about him in the present tense. At that time, his absence felt temporary. Dom couldn't help a hint of jealousy from creeping up as he watched Ms. Henry still able to hold her loved one so close.

"I'm sorry Elane gave you a tough time up front," Dom said as he walked them back to his office. "The way she spoke to you and threatened to call the police was inappropriate."

Ms. Henry raised an eyebrow. "Oh, we were going to see you today, regardless. Trust. You can't just run away thinking it's no big deal." Her last sentence was spoken inches from Jasmine's face. The occasional *ow* escaped Jasmine's mouth as her mom continued to pull her along.

Running away or running toward, Dom thought as they sat down. His desire to understand why Maurice might have run away from home had led him to research explaining that adolescents tend to run away from home because they're either leaving something they don't like or are going toward something they do. Sometimes it was a mix of both.

"Tell him where you were, Jasmine," Ms. Henry commanded.

"Hold on." Dom got up to set up Haven. They had been trained to only record the primary client, not relatives. Although it seemed unlikely Jasmine was going to say much, he didn't want to miss anything if she did. Plus, this could count as their second session, bringing them closer to utilizing the VR component. The blue light glowed to life again.

"Jasmine, I will sit here all day until you talk if I have to," Ms. Henry said. Jasmine turned away, looking at the headset to her left.

"How about you tell me how this all started, Ms. Henry," Dom said. "Jasmine, if you have anything to add just let me know, okay? We'll talk one-on-one afterward." Jasmine pulled her hood over her head, closing herself into a silent cocoon.

"It's this attitude right here, Mr. Dom." Ms. Henry pointed an accusatory finger at her daughter. "All I did was tell her to take the trash out and suddenly she was gone. I thought she got kidnapped or something, but the trash was still in the house. Turns out she just left. Now, she's gonna tell me she was at Jackson Park hanging with friends the whole time. For two days? Bullshit."

No movement from Jasmine.

"Did anything happen before this?" Dom asked. He thought back to the Henrys' intake form which indicated that Jasmine and her mom had a good relationship. Either something drastic happened or that description was off.

"You'd have to ask her," Ms. Henry replied. "Sometimes she's the Jasmine I've always known. Still innocent, asking me to remember to put chips on her sandwiches and stuff like that. But sometimes those teenage hormones take over and everything becomes a problem."

Dom knew there had to be a reason for Jasmine to run. Curiosity grew about where she had actually gone. It's hard for a young girl to survive out on the street for even just two days, so maybe she went somewhere other than the park or had someone with her to help her out. Dom checked in with Ms. Henry more about how she was feeling before asking to speak with Jasmine alone.

Dom moved his chair to try to get eye contact with Jasmine. She pulled her hood lower, to the tip of her nose. "Now that your mom's gone, you want to tell me what really happened?" More silence. Dom glanced at the Haven headset, wondering what it was analyzing with all the empty airspace. Why she left, where she went, who she was with, what she did, when might she run again. Every question came up with nothing.

He went over to his desk and grabbed a deck of Uno cards from a drawer. "Wanna play?" One eye opened and he got what looked like a shrug in return. "I bet I'll win." Dom dealt the cards, laying seven at Jasmine's feet. It only took a few solo rounds of him playing both of their cards and giving exaggerated reactions before she finally cracked.

"Really? You gotta do all that? I just wanna leave already," Jasmine said from under her hood.

"There's nothing stopping you from leaving," Dom said. Not here or at home, he thought to himself.

"I know my mom's right out there, probably trying to listen in," Jasmine shot back. "If she could, she'd lock me in here with you until she gets what she wants."

"And what's that?"

"How am I supposed to know?" The heat brewing inside Jasmine seemed to go beyond a threshold as she finally swept the hood from her head. With a scowl, she shook her head, appearing puzzled by her own question. Her eyes briefly met Dom's. "Ugh, stop sitting there just looking at me!" She kicked the deck of Uno cards, splaying them across the floor.

"I'm just trying to help, Jasmine," Dom said.

"I don't need help! I'd be better off if the police didn't find me," she snapped.

"And what would that have done to your mother?" His voice grew unexpectedly. "Do you have any idea what it's like for a family when someone goes missing? The long nights, worrying about the person's safety until it's been so long that you just have to give in and decide that they're probably—" he clenched his jaw to stop himself.

Jasmine looked at him with a disturbed expression. "I'm done with this."

EMBARRASSMENT HUNG ON DOM LIKE A HEAVY coat after the session and throughout the weekend. He'd gone overboard, letting his own experiences dictate how he talked to a client.

He'd stopped his own therapy in college because after a certain point it didn't make sense. He didn't have any grief to process, because he hadn't accepted Maurice's death.

His absence is still a loss. There's a lot of complicated emotions to manage related to this, his therapist would say.

The words became meaningless as he leaned into his desire to understand the why behind his cousin's disappearance. His parents were content with their conclusion about the situation, so he couldn't talk to them about the complex feelings brought up by his work with Jasmine. Kendra might understand, but they still hadn't spoken since the block party. Even the photos he sent her a few days back of the apartment he'd finally signed off on got no response.

Ms. Henry managed to drag Jasmine back to New Horizons on Monday for their scheduled appointment. Both looked serious. Jasmine stayed home over the weekend, due in no small part to what she called her mom's "lockdown." Dom applauded Ms. Henry internally, this time focused on controlling his reactions.

"You'll finally get to use this bad boy next week instead of having it here just as an ornament," he said, tapping the Haven headset.

Jasmine forced a smile. Her mom hadn't let her wear a hoodie this time so she would engage more in the session. "That's wonderful. I can't wait!" she said, smearing the sarcasm on heavily.

The session went better than the last. Probably because Dom decided not to ask Jasmine anything about running away. He wasn't going to let the issue go, he just figured he needed to regain some trust before addressing it again. Ms. Henry wouldn't like this approach, but she would have to trust him too.

He and Jasmine played multiple games of Uno throughout the hour as they talked about topics of her choice, mostly her favorite shows and movies she'd watched recently, before she was on lockdown, of course. The conversation was meant to be surface level, but he couldn't help trying to interpret what she shared to find potential motives behind her behaviors. Could watching a teen drama signal peer conflict in her life? A slasher reflect a hidden danger? He felt silly and a little manipulative thinking he could pull clues from their exchanges about pop culture. Perhaps he was more of a seasoned therapist than he thought.

"Still got it," Jasmine said as she slapped down her last card, winning for the third time in a row. "Thought I might be rusty after doing nothing but staring at the walls all weekend."

Dom raised an eyebrow, admiring her wit.

"So how exactly is this going to work?" Jasmine asked, pointing to the headset.

"We'll go over it again next week," Dom began, "but essentially after today, the Haven system is going to use the data from our first three sessions to create a virtual setting that will be most helpful for you. Then, we'll split the time in our remaining sessions between you starting with VR and then us discussing the experience afterwards. Sound okay?"

Jasmine nodded, her earlier sarcasm now mixed with seemingly genuine interest. "It's probably the closest thing to fun I'm going to have anytime soon."

Dom was equally eager to see Atlasal's creation prove its worth.

JULY

CHAPTER

NINE

THEY'RE COMING

The bright red letters bled deep into the cardboard sign. It had been almost a month since Dom accidentally kicked over the homeless man's cup of change. He had not seen the man since, or maybe just not noticed him, but he was unavoidable today. Sign in hand, the man stood in the middle of the sidewalk, his mass of coats making it look like he could have been hiding two people within them. Busy workers rushed around him like river water around a large rock.

Wanting to avoid another accident, Dom walked a wide radius around the man, nodding and giving a soft, "Good morning." He couldn't see through the shades the man had on and didn't pick up on any other signs of acknowledgement. He shrugged, continuing on his way to work.

Dom walked into the building wishing he could fast forward time. At noon, he would be meeting with Jasmine to use Haven's VR program for the first time. He started working with two other clients as well since Jasmine's emergency walk-in session, but they were still a couple weeks away from that phase of treatment.

Amalia greeted him in her office with a bright smile, matching his excitement. "This is great! You're going to do amazing!" It was a bit of an odd statement given that the Haven program would be doing most of the work. "Before we talk about Jasmine's case, I wanted to let you in on a little insider info," Amalia said. "Although initial standings in the Atlasal contest haven't been compiled yet, I was able to take a look at some of the data. Everyone now has a client they have started VR sessions with. Except Louis, he has two. Don't think of it as an advantage. It's possible Jasmine could make the same amount of improvement as his two clients combined."

Louis told Dom about the turn around he'd had with his second client deciding to consent to using Haven. He wondered why Amalia was framing the information as secret when the contest leaderboard was going to contain even more data about how each therapist at the clinic was performing. He recalled the conversation he'd overheard, wondering if Amalia was trying to prod him in some way to pick up his efforts. He wanted to meet Miranda Webb, but did Amalia want him to win the contest, too? Was it okay for her to have a horse in the race?

"Time to get to work, then," Dom said.

"Let's make sure Jasmine starts off strong." Amalia pulled up the Haven analysis of their first three sessions on her laptop as Dom did the same on his tablet. "Let's go over this one more time."

Even after seeing it multiple times, he was still overtaken with wonder at the narrative summary of the sessions. Things had changed so quickly with Jasmine over the course of two weeks. From the initial referral regarding school avoidance to the running away incident, it was fascinating to see what the computer program came up with.

The connection between the client's desires to evade both school and home calls for further exploration. While the school avoidance had a clear impetus, the absconding behavior appears to be unmotivated at this time. It is hypothesized that an underlying anxiety...

"How do you feel about the virtual environment created by Haven?" Amalia asked.

Along with the narrative summary, the program attached a one-minute snippet of the VR setting it had generated through its analysis. Clicking on the video again, Dom watched the scene unfold. An Atlasal logo faded, revealing the opening to a forest. The camera pushed its way into the tall trees. Even through the screen, it felt immersive, like being inside of a wooded fortress. Like nothing outside of the forest existed, the canopy a gently rustling roof.

The caption under the video explained that the setting was designed for meditative practice, inviting exploration in a contained environment. It intentionally did not resemble anything in Jasmine's actual surroundings as a means of allowing her to feel a sense of distance from her typical experiences and perhaps the sources of her distress. Giving her a little bit of what she wanted, it seemed. Being away from it all.

"I was expecting something more elaborate at first," Dom said. "But this is what the system recommended, so I won't argue with it."

"Yeah, David said they were intentional about the data used to train Haven, because they didn't want it to create any fantastical environments that didn't make sense for mental health care," Amalia reminded him. "What are your ideas on how you'll integrate Jasmine's initial VR time in the rest of the session?"

"I want to know what she gets out of the virtual experience. How she feels being in a place that's nothing like her home or school. Like the summary says, I really want to understand what it is that provoked her to run away and want to stay out there."

Dom had not told Amalia about his personal connection to the issue. When she had reviewed the recording of the walk-in session and heard his outburst, he explained it away. "You know, like all those true crime documentaries about kidnappings. The kids' families are always so torn up, I guess I kinda laid into her because she wasn't seeing the risks," he had said.

"Great, I think that's a good plan. Don't want to get too deep yet. And remember this VR thing is a new experience for both of you. There will be an adjustment. It's worth making sure you're both comfortable rather than focusing on the progress being measured. Well, you know what I mean." It was like for a short time she reverted to her natural self, forgetting she was supposed to hype the competition.

Dom basically rushed Jasmine and Ms. Henry down the hall to his office when they finally arrived. Ms. Henry said it had been a pretty good week with Jasmine, with only one argument coming up between them. It was the first time Jasmine had a genuine smile on her face before the session. Her anticipation seemed just as high as Dom's.

She darted straight to the Haven headset as soon as she stepped through the office door. "Hold on, now," Dom said. "We need to review some things before you get started." He tapped some buttons on the headset and his tablet to start up the VR program.

"I know, you told me everything last week," Jasmine said. "I've used VR before, anyway. I'm not new to this."

"We didn't go over everything yet," Dom said. "I'm pretty sure this will be different from other VR you've used. Let me tell you about the virtual environment you'll be exploring today." He told her about the forest setting and how a copy of his voice would guide her through calming, meditative exercises. She squinted back at him, looking doubtful. "Maybe not as fun as a video game, but it will help us keep moving forward with therapy."

Jasmine hopped up from her chair, grabbing the headset. "Come on, let's go!"

Dom put a hand out, motioning for her to slow down. "Okay, last thing," he said as he tapped another button on his tablet. "I'll be able to see everything you're seeing on my screen here in real time," he explained, waving the tablet. "You let me know if you have any problems in there. And even though you'll be sitting, if you feel dizzy or just want to stop for whatever reason, don't hesitate."

Jasmine mockingly saluted. "Got it. I don't think this thing will give me any issues. Atlasal can do it all, right?" she said, reciting one of the company's popular taglines while tapping the logo on the side of the headset.

Dom helped Jasmine put on the device, gently tightening the band around her braids. Then he handed her the two hand controls needed for moving around the VR setting. He sat across from her and hit "START" on his tablet. He placed an earphone into his left ear so he could hear the same thing as Jasmine as the program started.

"Hello, Jasmine," he heard his voice say. It was eerie hearing the re-creation of his voice come up with words of its own.

"Today, you're going to be starting a new adventure." Dom caught something off in the pronunciation of the last word, sounding more like two words: ad venture. Maybe the voice copying process had some flaws. *"In this cozy forest, you're going to learn how to leave all your worries behind."* A path leading to an opening in the forest slowly came into view on his tablet.

"Step right on in." The point of view pushed forward, jittering a bit from side to side as Jasmine played with the controls. She continued further until she reached a small glade. Dom marveled at the quality of the rendering. Tall columns of bark encircled the camera, protective guards with leafy canopies acting as shields to the outside world.

"In this first exercise, you'll be introduced to a grounding technique that we'll continue to use in the coming weeks. As you stand in the middle of the clearing, leaves will begin gently falling. You don't need to count them, just observe. The color of the leaves will change as the exercise continues. Don't worry about remembering all of the colors, simply note the change. The idea is to practice paying attention to your environment. Afterwards, we'll talk about how you can use this technique in your daily life."

A single leaf drifted down, sliding and twisting through the air. As more followed from above the screen, Dom looked at Jasmine. From the nose down, her face seemed free of tension. Her breathing was slowing. Coming up with a similar mindfulness technique himself would have been easy. He had used several grounding exercises with clients while interning, but it seemed Jasmine was engaging with this one much faster.

The leaves shifted from green to yellow, and a few oranges were beginning to appear when Dom's tablet screen froze. He tapped it a few times, then looked up at Jasmine again. Everything seemed normal for a few seconds until her neck jumped back like when someone accidently walks into a spider web.

"What?" She sounded confused.

"Who?" A hint of fear crept into her voice.

"Oh, unh-unh." She began grabbing at the headband.

Dom hopped up, helping her remove the headset. "What happened?" he asked. "My screen froze, so I couldn't see anything."

"I don't know, something weird is going on. Like a glitch. Look," she motioned for Dom to put on the headset.

Standing, he adjusted the headband and placed the device over his eyes. His mouth hung open as he took in the scene. The falling leaves had been replaced by stark white pieces of paper. They were dropping at a faster rate, as if being tossed down from the lowest tree branch. Focusing through the flurry, the words appearing in bold red ink on each piece became decipherable.

THEY'RE COMING.

He instinctively stepped back from the growing pile of paper, forgetting he was in a virtual environment and tripped over his chair. He felt Jasmine's hand on his back, helping to break his fall. When he removed the headset, he looked at her with a matching face full of confusion. "Um, let's take a quick break, okay. Why don't you go sit with your mom while I figure out what's going on with the system."

Once Jasmine left, Dom sat, his heart still pumping fast, his breathing beginning to slow back down. The headset rested on the chair across from him. He got the strange feeling that the device was watching him. Leaning over, he jabbed the power button off. He had played video games most of his life, but had never seen a glitch like what Haven just produced.

The back of his neck tingled as the message on the pieces of paper stayed fixed in his mind. He knew the homeless man's sign that morning had said the same thing, but he couldn't allow himself to see it as more than a coincidence. If it were, that would mean the glitch was more than just a glitch.

"I'm probably overthinking it," he muttered.

He grabbed his tablet and scrolled through the Haven menu. It recorded each VR session for reviewing purposes. The timestamp on the video he pulled up indicated it had captured Jasmine's entire session despite freezing on his screen. He fast forwarded to the grounding exercise. The leaves fell, green and then yellow. As oranges started to mix in, there was a slight hiccup in the visual, but it continued as it should have. All orange leaves fell to the ground until the video came to an end. No one would be able to see what he and Jasmine had.

Despite not wanting to fall behind in New Horizons' contest, he also didn't want Jasmine to experience another "technical difficulty" until he knew Haven would function properly.

Dom brought Jasmine back into the room to check on her. She had only told her mom that the headset wasn't working right. "I'll have this thing figured out by next week," he said, placing the headset on his desk, "but let's finish our session."

"What was that? You sure it can get fixed?" She still sounded a little scared, but also disappointed by the possibility she wouldn't be able to use the headset again.

"Computers mess up sometimes," he replied with a shrug, trying to come off nonchalant. He wondered if notifying Atlasal about the issue was worth it. Maybe he would just let their tech support know there was a problem without getting into the details. "Tell me, before whatever that was happened, how did you like the exercise?"

"Um, it was okay," she said.

"You seemed pretty relaxed."

"Yeah, I really felt like I was in the forest. I don't think I've seen one like that before, so it was cool." Her attention seemed to drift inward.

"You're right, we don't have trees like that around here. Especially not the kind with leaves that change color in mid-air," he said, trying to lighten the mood in the room. No reaction from Jasmine. "Are there any ways you think you could use a similar grounding technique at home?"

"Hmm, I could stare at the wall in my bedroom and count the number of times my mom comes in to make sure I haven't left again." She looked at him with a straight face.

Dom was surprised, yet pleased, to hear her bring up the running away topic on her own. "Sounds rough." He paused, letting the statement hang between them, hoping it would show he had the ability to see things from her perspective.

"Like, I get she doesn't trust me, but I can't stay inside forever. What am I supposed to do when I'm stressed out?" She frowned to one side, dragging her eyes to the floor.

Dom had worked with children and teens enough to know their stressors were valid, so he dug for more information. "What gets you so stressed that you need time away?"

Jasmine shrugged. "I don't know. Normal stuff, I guess. My mom thinks the lockdown at school was this big thing that changed me forever, but she just didn't listen to me before about all the other things going on in my life. So, I just let it all build up."

This was the most context Dom received so far. It brought the school lockdown back into the picture in a way he hadn't expected. It seemed like that incident was just the most recent and maybe most severe stressor Jasmine was trying to manage. He wanted to dive deeper, but knew he had to pace himself for her to open up more.

That afternoon before leaving work he checked in with Amalia about the glitch. "It was like the simulation was changing to something completely different. Maybe the program was mixing in elements from whatever the next lesson is that it has prepared." He didn't mention the bright red message.

Amalia sighed, looking frustrated. He couldn't tell if it was at him or not. "This is not good." She took a deep breath, speaking in a rushed cadence. "I'll pass the concern along to Atlasal. I may check with David as well to see if there's some way you can get a weighted score for this session since you can't expect to see quality progress with a broken system." Irritation left its footprints on her face.

When he left her office, Dom stood just outside the door for a minute. He heard another heavy sigh from Amalia. He only caught the tail end of what she said next, as her voice sounded muffled by her hands. "... gonna do to me? Ugh."

CHAPTER

TEN

Downtown was alive.

It seemed like half the city was out and about, enjoying the still, Saturday evening summer air. Enticing smells wafted from restaurants. Bouncing playlists and boozy chatter clashed as they left bar windows. Most of the people in these establishments would not have dared venture over to Dom's side of town due to whatever stories they'd heard about it. He felt just as out of place as he weaved between people on the sidewalk, head down while trying to follow his phone's GPS to what was a new destination for him. A red dot on his screen marked Prime Rose Gallery: the spot where Kendra was having her first art exhibit.

Things had gotten weird fast at work and it felt worse not being able to share any of it with her. He wanted her to know what he'd seen in the headset. She was the only one who would understand his suspicion, given their strange run-ins with other Atlasal products.

The light was dim as he entered the gallery. A poster on the wall read: H.O.M.E: Honoring Our Many Experiences—a Kendra Walker creation. Each time he had seen the exhibit's name on Kendra's social media pages, he smiled. Despite what he said about her choice in career, Dom had always been wowed by her creativity.

Nate waved as Dom stepped into the exhibit space. He gave a half-hearted wave back, not to be rude, but because his attention was completely consumed by the scene before him. The wall in front of him was lined with painted portraits. The faces of children, men, and women stared, smiled, and mean-mugged back at him. He recognized some of them, but all were depicted in front of backgrounds of various parts of Parkside. It was a small, yet powerful selection of the people who shaped him. The people he cared about. The people he worked hard to protect. There was already a decent sized crowd at the event, moseying around and taking in the art. He wondered how many of them felt the same commitment to the people in the portraits.

"What's good?" Nate dapped up Dom. It was the first time Dom had ever seen him wear a turtleneck. If the idea was to look more cultured, Dom wasn't buying it. "You actually showed up."

"There's no do not allow list, right?" Dom said. "I told you I wasn't going to let Kendra ghost me out of seeing her first exhibit." He looked back and forth. "Have you seen her yet?"

"Yeah, she's somewhere around here schmoozing with the guests, doing her artist thing," Nate said.

They walked around the portrait wall into another section of the gallery. Dom stopped in his tracks again. Suspended from the ceiling, the canvas from the block party displayed the hand and footprints of the kids from that day. Although he had witnessed part of its making, the finished product was striking. The way the kids' markings rose and dipped with the waves of the hanging material created a sense of movement. These were kids navigating and shaping their environment. Standing beneath the amazing piece, Kendra was surrounded by a cluster of guests.

She was in her element. She glided back and forth between guests, her blue dress flowing out from under a stylish leather jacket. As she exchanged words, her head would periodically toss back in laughter, sending her curls into a bouncing waterfall. Dom knew her well enough to know these weren't the forced laughs of someone trying to impress an art afficionado; Kendra was truly having the time of her life as she talked to people about her work.

He walked in closer. He caught the tail end of her comment to a short, black-haired woman in bright pink overalls. "...allowing the kids to create in their own way. I had so much fun just watching them do it." He stood off to the side of the petite woman, giving them privacy but intentionally entering Kendra's line of view. After some more words and a little chuckle, the woman walked off.

"You're here," she said matter-of-factly, stepping over to him.

"I figured it's not crashing if it's open to the public. I'm not in these bougie parts much, but I found my way."

A small smirk flashed on her face. "I thought you'd have more important things to do than coming to an art show."

He shook his head. "Wouldn't miss this for the world. Your talent is crazy. Those portraits over there?" He pointed his thumb behind him, his eyes wide with astonishment.

"I appreciate it," she said bluntly. "So, how have things been with you?"

Seeing how much Kendra was thriving in the moment of the exhibit, he didn't want to get too deep into his own issues. "Good. Work has been...interesting."

"That video game therapy solve the world's problems yet?"

"Virtual reality has presented some challenges so far," he said. "That always happens when using tech in new ways, though. My clients really seem to like it."

"That's good," she said dryly.

Dom bit down on the inside of his cheek. Before he could decide what to say next, a self-important looking man came up and whispered in Kendra's ear.

"Look, I have to go give my speech," she said. "I'm going to introduce a special piece. Just remember that all is fair in art, okay?"

"Umm, okay," he replied with a shrug.

The guests were directed to gather in the center of the gallery. Dom and Nate stood toward the back of the group as something boxy and covered in a white sheet was wheeled in. Kendra stood next to it with a microphone in her hand.

"Thank you all so much for coming out to my very first art exhibit," she began. Applause rounded the room. "H.O.M.E. is a project I feel like I've been working on my whole life. I'm from this city. It made me who I am, in all the best ways, of course," she ran her hand through her hair, dramatically tossing it back to a swell of laughter. "With as much pride as I have though, I still feel like my home is a secret. Sure, people know Selton for different industries and stuff like that, but who really knows *us*?" She spread her arms, encompassing the art that represented her people. Her gaze seemed to hang on Dom a little longer than others as she scanned the room. "Real people really live here, and I want everyone to know that. That's why I put everything I could into these pieces. Literally. The portraits when you enter the gallery use paints that have extracts from local native plants mixed in. The people are made up of the place. The two can't be separated." She paused, taking a deep breath. A calmness had swept the audience as everyone took in her words. The truth in them moved Dom in a way he hadn't expected.

Kendra placed a hand on the white sheet next to her. "This last piece I wanted to save to share with you all more directly. It's my first work of sculpture art, so I think I was a little nervous to just have it out on display, but it also holds a lot of personal meaning I want to explain first." A gulp echoed through the microphone. "Home is a relationship. How you treat it is important. At times you love it. At others, it angers you. You work to make it better. You feel the need to protect it. If you ever leave it and come back, you will realize it's not the same. But what changed more? It, or you?"

She pulled the sheet down, pushing it behind her with her foot. She stood back a few feet with her head down, allowing the guests to look at the piece. Dom and Nate had to wait for the first cluster of people to move on before they could get a full view. Inside of a clear, rectangular display, a tall piece of glass divided the space in two. On one side, a replica of downtown Selton City stood. On the other was a gold human figurine, looking like a trophy removed from its base. A small placard read, "Golden Child," with arrows pointed away from each other, directing people to look at the display from both ends. The curvature of the dividing glass provided the perspective for spectators to decipher. From the side of the gold figurine, the city became an even smaller model of itself. From the side of the city, the gold man similarly shrunk down by half.

"I don't get it," Nate said. "A little too artsy for me."

Dom, however, seethed as the meaning sunk in for him. He stayed behind after Nate left, waiting for the crowd to thin out as the exhibit got closer to its end time. Once only a few people remained, he pulled Kendra over by the restrooms. He had mulled over what to say, but still struggled to organize a sentence out of the chaos running through his mind. They hadn't had a normal, friendly conversation since he got back home, and now it seemed like getting back to normal was further off than ever.

"What's really going on?" he asked, waving a hand in the direction of the sculpture.

Kendra looked annoyed. "That's the main reason I didn't invite you. I knew you wouldn't understand."

"Oh, I understand. You think I'm a goddamn megalomaniac who sees himself as more important than everyone else, but I'm really a nobody once you put things in perspective. Am I close?"

"It's just an expression of my feelings, Dom. My experience."

"This place is my home, too, you know? I'm trying to help in my own way, and all you're doing is making me out to look like some kinda wannabe savior." His anger simmered. "You act like I did something personal to you. What did I do?"

Kendra's jaw muscles pulsed as she tried to hold back.

"You ran away, too!" Spittle flew from her mouth as tears simultaneously burst from her face. "Just like Maurice!"

His eye twitched, taken back by the mention of Maurice and confused by Kendra's show of emotion. "What are you talking about?"

"After he disappeared, you did, too," she said, catching her breath between sobs. "It just took longer. Of course, I know you were hurting. *Are* hurting. But you just kept withdrawing, and when you decided to go to school all the way across the country, it felt like a final decision. Like you wouldn't come back and you were okay with leaving me behind. That's not what you do to a friend. Sure, you're back now, but not really. Not all the way."

Dom's head was spinning. He couldn't believe what he was hearing. None of it made sense. "Wow. You really are talented. The way you just twisted everything I went through with Maurice into being about you—that's art." Furious, he stormed out of the gallery, leaving Kendra with her face buried in the sleeve of her leather jacket.

The dark night met Dom. He didn't pay attention to where he was going; he didn't care as long as it was away from Kendra. Frustration carried his feet forward. How could she judge him while at the same time acknowledging what he had been through? Their friendship was never this tumultuous and he didn't know what to do about it.

A gust of wind sent an aluminum can scraping across the sidewalk in front of him. He looked up and for the first time since leaving the gallery, he stopped. A few yards in front of him, wearing a black trench coat flowing in the wind, stood the homeless man. The red-lettered sign and the message in the Haven program flashed through Dom's mind. He was far away from the man's usual corner by New Horizons. Taking in his surroundings, he found himself on a quiet street with no cars. The only other people, a couple on the other side of the street, had just turned a corner and were now out of sight.

"What do you want?" Dom yelled, hoping his voice would carry to the couple or someone else nearby.

The man took a step forward.

Dom took one back.

"I've seen you before. I think you know that. Are you following me?" Dom asked, adding more bass to his voice.

"No," rolled out from the man's mouth, with a gravelly tone. He took his hands out of his coat pockets, turning them over to show they were empty. "I ain't gonna hurt ya."

A now obvious realization struck Dom. "Are you with Atlasal? Did they pay you?" That must be why the man's sign matched the glitch. It was all planned.

The man snorted a sharp laugh.

His heart beating in his throat, Dom turned quickly to run across the street. "Help!"

He got only a few strides off the sidewalk before the man had the back of his shirt tight in his grasp. The man was much faster than Dom thought someone his age would be. The man's arms wrapped around him, his hold showcasing a musculature that also seemed out of place. Dom struggled to get free, finding it increasingly hard to take in a breath to yell for help again. A black cloth came up to his nose and mouth, the night swallowing him as his vision blurred then faded into nothing.

CHAPTER

ELEVEN

"This is him?"

"...a little overboard don't you think?"

"You sure he's ready?"

He felt his breath returning under his control. Upon opening his eyes, the floor started to spin. He quickly shut them. Through the wooziness, he could tell he was sitting, so at least he wouldn't fall over. Hoping to rub some focus into his eyes, he realized he couldn't move his arms. Dom's eyes shot back open.

Looking down, he saw ropes wrapped around him securing his arms, chest, and legs to a metal chair. The room around him continued to rock like a ship in a storm, but he was able to pick up some details: exposed walls, wooden beams, and a bench all illuminated by a bright fluorescent light.

"Agh." The bulb above his head sent blotches of color through his vision. "Heeey!" he screamed at the top of his lungs. "Where am I?! ... Anybody there? ... Help!" He looked left and right, frantically trying to find the man who'd taken him. From behind, beyond where he could turn to see, steps approached.

Searing against the dingy background of wherever he was, a blaze of colorful robes swooped into view, reds, oranges, and yellows dancing over the ground as if knowing that even a slight graze of the concrete would displease the person donning them. A matching head wrap punctuated the authoritative look of the woman who stared back at Dom.

"You're awake I see." She dragged the small, cushioned bench over and sat. "Apologies for the rough tactics used to get you here. I never would have approved of it if anyone had run it by me." Her eyes softened, as if trying to comfort him.

His heart was racing. "Who are you? A- Are you with the ho- homeless guy? Where am I?" He blinked hard, attempting to reset the scene in front of him. "Damn it. You're with Atlasal, too, right? Why are they doing this? Why me?"

"Uuugh. I can't take it. If this is the extent of his analytical skills, I don't know why we dragged him here." The unfamiliar voice came from behind and to the right of Dom.

The woman in front of him shot a glare in that direction, her eyes wide with rebuke. "No, no, we're not

Atlasal or any type of affiliate," she said. "Again, this isn't the way I wanted this introduction to happen," she glanced intently behind Dom, "but here we are."

If this person, these people, weren't working with Atlasal, then who were they? What did they plan to do with him? As the whirling motion of the room slowed, his mind began to spin internally, trying to figure out how he'd ended up in this situation.

"My name is Axel." She spoke with conviction. Maybe Dom's perception was still off from whatever was used to knock him out, but her name seemed to echo around the room for an inordinate amount of time.

"My group here is made up of people dedicated to helping," she said.

"What?" Dom asked. She was being too vague. "How does kidnapping and tying me up help anything?"

"Just be straight with the boy already," the unknown voice spoke again. "I'm tired of typing all these question marks."

Dom scrunched his face in confusion.

Axel pressed her lips together impatiently. "Francis back there is our archivist. Amongst many other things, he keeps records of our important meetings. Including when we have a new recruit."

"Recruit? A recruit for what?" Dom asked. "Wait, an archivist? Like a librarian? Is that where we are?" He looked around again, trying to spot any clues within his limited field of view.

"Don't even try it," Francis chirped, quick footsteps carrying him closer. A man in a half-buttoned, band collared guayabera came in from the right, gripping a tablet under his arm. A single chain swung in and out of his shirt as he spoke theatrically. "No shade to the librarians, but I am a keeper of knowledge, a holder of legacies, and a—"

"Please, Francis," Axel said, clasping her hands together. "Not now. I'll get to the point." She took a deep breath as Francis took a few steps back, remaining in Dom's sight. He noticed arrow and diamond-shaped designs cut into Francis' fade as he shook his head.

"What I mean by helping is healing. Our group acts to further the well-being of all African peoples, wherever they may be. One of our earliest names was The People of the Hills, but we are now simply known as The Village." Again, her words sent an energy pulsing through the room.

Dom furrowed his brow.

"No," Francis held a hand out. "Please, no more questions. Just listen."

"Let me start from the beginning," Axel said. She put her shoulders back, sitting up in a regal posture. "Since before the Maafa, what you know as the Atlantic Slave Trade, our progenitors held important positions in their communities. People now may call them shamans, witch doctors, or otherwise, but they were healers. Leaders. Of course, that all changed once we were torn from our homes and forced to do the work of beasts. Under those conditions, it was obvious that our people were in need. But so many had forgotten the old ways. Who could blame them? It was often too difficult to even think about anything other than making it to the next day. For some, however, this led to a clear choice. They chose to flee."

"You mean, like, maroons?" Dom asked.

Francis looked up with a raised eyebrow. "Oh, so he does know a little something?"

"Yes," Axel responded. "Throughout the regions where we were held captive—North, South, and Central America, the Caribbean—small pockets of resistance began to form as more took hold of their freedom. The healers were at the forefront of those who came to be known as maroons, leading the way out and encouraging others to join them. They knew that liberation was the greatest salve for their brethren. As some of these groups stumbled upon each other, or heard colonizers complaining of escaped property, an understanding grew that there were many of us out there. A network began to form that still exists today."

Logically, Dom knew maroon descendants were alive today, but Axel's story didn't make sense. Maroon descendants were not a clandestine group and certainly didn't search around for "recruits." They were simply part of an historical legacy of those who escaped slavery and formed independent communities. "You're telling me that the maroons formed a secret society across the Western Hemisphere that is still connected today. How?"

"Correction, we span the entire globe now. And, not every maroon or descendant was or is part of The Village," Axel explained. "Neither does every current member of The Village have to be a maroon descendant. Nowadays, we are joined by those willing to support our cause. This is a point of contention amongst some Village hubs. You see, there is no overarching structure or governing body of The Village. It is easier to survive in this nebulous form. The loss of one leader doesn't eliminate us."

Dom had so many questions, but needed one thing addressed first. "So, it's safe to assume the guy who brought me here isn't really homeless. He's one of you." Axel's face twitched slightly. "But, you guys still have to be connected to Atlasal in some way because he had a sign that—"

"Ooh, ooh, my turn, boss! Please, let me show off my work!" An airy voice came from behind Dom and to the left, again out of sight.

Axel sighed. "Show off your work? You mean your failed attempt that led to our guest being brought here unconscious?" She paced back and forth, looking annoyed. Shaking her head she said, "Okay, Charles. Cut the top rope. Let him see all of us."

A new set of footsteps approached from directly behind Dom. A heavy hand dropped onto his right shoulder. "Stay still now." The rough scratch of a knife went down the back of the chair until the rope went slack from around his arms and torso. Finally, he was able to move more freely. Before he even thought about trying to untie his legs, he saw who had cut his top half free.

A man in a white t-shirt that gripped his muscular arms towered over him. He had four thick locs so long they extended down to where his camo pants met the top of his black boots. "Yeah, I wouldn't try nothing if I was you," he said, revealing a mouth of gold teeth. Echoes of a Louisiana upbringing lived in his voice.

"Would you stop trying to scare him?"

Dom looked the other way, now able to see the woman who interjected earlier.

Sitting with three computer monitors behind her, a young, brown-skinned woman with two afro puffs smiled. "Charles is more bark than bite," she said, winking from behind large-framed glasses with her left eye, which was surrounded by a splash of pale skin.

"Hmph." Charles went back to his original spot, sitting on a crate. He rested his hand on the butt of a rifle balanced next to him. Dom breathed in sharply.

"Only a replica, dude. Like I said." The woman imitated the bark of a small dog then flashed another smile. "I'm Nille by the way. I'm the one behind the little mishap in the headset," she said, waving her hand with a flourish at the screens behind her. "Sorry your client got scared in the process, but it had to be done."

"You said you're supposed to look out for people's well-being. You're a group of healers," Dom said, looking back at Axel. "How is hacking a part of that?"

Nille crossed her arms. "Find a gap in the defenses around an operating system and then exploit it so you can alter the functions of said system. Sounds a lot like one of your little therapy sessions to me."

Francis chuckled approvingly.

Axel jumped in, "We haven't been able to make sense of the details yet, but we have a hunch Atlasal is up to something. There's a lot to keep track of to keep Selton City secure, cut Atlasal's intrusion is quite intriguing. Our first clues came from the video footage Nille acquisitioned from an Atlasal drone."

"Wait, I think I had a run-in with the same drone. The guys flying it work for Atlasal. How'd you get footage from them?" Dom asked.

"I'm pretty convincing," Nille chimed in. "I'd seen them doing test flights at the park. I just nerded out to them enough to let me hold the drone, and then used a special device to wirelessly download the footage."

"The drone mostly just circled Parkside and surrounding neighborhoods," Axel explained. "We also got our hands on the scooter that ran through the block party. Whether it initially had a rider or not, it was definitely tracing a specific path. Like it was being directed."

What could that mean? Unease creeped into Dom's mind. He'd been resisting turning the incidents into more than coincidences, but people he'd never met until tonight were raising concerns about the same things.

"And this all made you hack into Atlasal's system?" he asked.

"An associate figured out the connection between the drone pilots and New Horizons, and thus their deal with Atlasal. In order to start piecing things together, we needed to contact someone on the inside," Axel explained.

"The hack was a rushed job, admittedly," Nille said. "I know 'They're coming' is super vague. My work is usually way more elegant, but I'd say this one was still effective in terms of getting your attention."

Dom thought about the falling scraps of paper and the cardboard sign. Knowing who was behind it didn't help shake the shock of the moment. "Ok, so you're not working with Atlasal. But, back to the homeless guy. Why has he been tracking *me*? You guys could have chosen anyone else at New Horizons to help you."

"Dom..." Axel hesitated. It didn't faze him that she knew his name, being that he had been tracked for weeks before being literally kidnapped. "I'm not the one who can tell you that."

Francis angled a wide-eyed glance at her. Nille rotated back to her screens, trying to hide her reaction. Charles didn't budge.

Axel nervously scratched under her headwrap before yelling out, "Alright! You can come down now!"

From the distance, Dom heard footsteps descending an unseen staircase. The steps were measured, as if the person were following a count. Emerging from around a corner, Dom saw the homeless man whom he now knew was clearly something else. The man came to stand next to Axel, his presence backing Francis back into the corner he had initially been in.

"He can explain himself," Axel said. This was the first thing she had said where she didn't sound confident or sure of herself. Something in her tone sounded worried.

The man was in the same outfit he had on when he kidnapped Dom, but the light of the room gave the clearest view of him yet. Without the usual pile of coats surrounding him, Dom noticed the man's rigid posture. His afro was still dirty, but the dust somehow seemed even, like it had been placed there. Dom studied his face trying to figure out the man's age in relation to how strong he seemed during their struggle. He guessed the man was somewhere in his forties until he noticed something. A line on the man's neck, distinguishing different shades of brown skin, but not like a tan.

"I'm glad you're sitting down," the man said, his voice not as rough as before. "I'm not sure either of us is ready for this." The man grabbed a clump of his hair and pulled, stretching his forehead in a grotesque manner, followed by his eyes, nose, and the rest of his face until he removed the mask.

Dom immediately felt hollow inside, like everything had collapsed into an internal black hole, as he looked back into the eyes of his cousin, Maurice.

Out of the void rushed five years' worth of emotion. A cry-scream projected from his mouth, his body shaking uncontrollably. The unfathomability of the moment was so heavy that he toppled his chair over, slamming into the concrete.

When the man—Maurice—came over to pick him up, Dom reeled at his touch, not out of revulsion, but out of disbelief that what was happening was real. His cousin, gone for so long, was face-to-face with him.

Dom tried to regain his composure. "I- is…is it…"

"Yes, it's really me," Maurice replied. "It was me the whole time, cuz."

"But, how?"

"Between all the coats and this mask here," Maurice said, holding up the lifeless face next to his, "it was pretty easy to stay undercover."

Axel loudly cleared her throat.

"Sorry, right." Maurice rubbed his bald head then stuck his hands in his pockets. "How am I here. Alive. I have The Village to thank for that." He paused. "The day I left home I didn't really have a plan."

Dom was immediately transported back to that day. If not looking for drugs, maybe Maurice had just gone out for a long walk, his parents had thought early on, trying to stay positive. Maybe he had met up with friends somewhere in the city. As midnight had approached on the second day and no one they reached out to had seen Maurice, the mood in the house shifted.

"I didn't intend to runaway necessarily," Maurice continued. "I just knew I couldn't go back yet. There was too much pain in Parkside. And nothing—not even the pills I tried here and there—could get rid of it. By the time a few days passed, the cops hadn't found me, and I was still in one piece, I figured I could stay out there."

"I knew you were going through a lot," Dom said. "But I don't get how running away, or whatever you want to call it, was supposed to help anything. We took you in. My parents did so much for you!" He smacked the side of the chair with the last word.

"It wasn't enough, Dom. They couldn't provide what I really needed."

Dom balled his fists. If his legs weren't still tied, he would have got up and punched his cousin in the jaw.

"I know that's hard to hear," Maurice continued. "But it's the truth. I needed answers that you and your parents didn't have. Answers to questions some of which I didn't even know I had. Axel was the first Villager I met. She spotted me at a convenience store a little bit outside of town. She recognized me from the news, but she chose to just listen to my story."

"Wait! You knew he was missing and didn't do anything? Didn't notify anyone?" Dom yelled at Axel.

"Again, The Village is about healing," Axel said. "Of course I wanted to help him. He wasn't in the best shape at the time. Tired, hungry, scared. But after listening to him, it was clear that continuing the life he was living wouldn't help. I did only what he asked of me."

"Bullshit! You knew what you were doing was wrong." Dom stood and began wrestling with the rope around his calves. "Once Mom and Dad hear about this—"

"No!" Maurice grabbed Dom by the shoulders and pushed him back down into the chair. "You're not telling them shit. I've been a ghost for five years; you think I can't disappear again? You tell anyone I'm alive, how are you gonna prove it? You try to take any pictures, Nille can easily scrub your phone. Everybody will just think you're crazy."

It had only taken a year before any suggestion from Dom that Maurice was still out there was met by his parents with contempt. It was like bringing up the possibility disrupted their chosen grief. Maurice was right. "What am I supposed to do?" he asked. "These last five years have been torture. If I have to keep this secret, I'll lose my mind."

"You're going to keep it together. We'll help," Maurice said, looking around at the rest of The Village. "It might not feel like it, but whatever's going on with Atlasal is bigger than you and me right now. Nille, tell him."

"Is it safe to speak now?" Nille removed the earbuds she had put in. "Quite the fiery family reunion we have here."

"Nille, please," Maurice said.

"Okay, okay," she said, putting her hands up. "Aaaanyway." She shifted, looking at Dom. "Your girl Miranda Webb is coming to town soon. Early August."

"I thought September was when she was coming to meet the winner of New Horizons' contest," Dom said.

"Well, a little birdie that got access to her emails told me different," Nille said with a smirk. "Webb is making a preliminary trip to meet with Selton City's mayor. Something about finalizing details on a project. What we need you to do is find out what that project is."

Dom was dumbfounded. "And how am I supposed to do that?"

"Remember that little technologically gifted birdie I just mentioned?" Nille asked playfully. "I'm gonna use it to fabricate some emails telling Webb to leave a USB containing these project details with your CEO, Stacy Connors. You swipe it from her office, and we find out what they're up to."

Dom thought about the implications of stealing from his new employer. "What if I don't do it?"

"We don't get involved with trivial matters, Dom," Axel answered. "This situation raises enough flags for us to take seriously. You should do the same."

"Dom, if you don't agree to this, I'll have to cut ties again." Maurice's expression was serious. "If you want to understand anything more about the past five years, I need you to do this for me. For The Village."

"You ran away, too!"

Kendra's words rang through Dom's head. His disagreement with her statement was even clearer now. The evidence of how different his and Maurice's actions were stood right in front of him.

Dom struggled to accept that Maurice could so easily threaten to run out of his life again. He needed to make sense of who the person standing in front of him was now. And to do that he needed time.

"Okay. I'll do it."

CHAPTER
TWELVE

His stomach felt like it was turning inside out when he saw "Mom" come up on his phone. Back in his own bed, only one thing ran through his mind.

Maurice.

It was all he wanted to talk about when he answered the phone on the fifth ring. "There you are. Late night I assume?" she asked.

"Maurice is alive! He's joined this underground organization called The Village that is forcing me to steal information from my job!"

"Uh, yeah," was all he could allow himself to say. "I went to Kendra's art show."

He cared enough about maintaining contact with Maurice to not mention last night's events. What he wasn't sure of yet was how much Maurice cared about him. After five years apart, it seemed their only shared concern was the inner workings of Atlasal, not the damage done to their family by Maurice's absence. He hated that Atlasal was a bargaining chip between them.

"Oh! So, you two patched things up?"

"No. She thinks I abandoned her like Maurice abandoned us. Who, by the way, is alive! Like I always knew."

Instead, he shared, "Not quite. There's still some stuff we have to work through."

"Well, I know you will, but I'll stop bothering you about it. Just called to check on you."

Dom struggled to continue the mundane conversation, gratefully hanging up minutes later. If he could, he would have stayed huddled in his apartment for the next month, until The Village needed him to carry out the robbery. He wanted to avoid the weirdness that had entered his life as much as possible, but he had to maintain a normal presence at New Horizons.

Ms. Henry and Jasmine did not show for the scheduled Monday morning appointment. Dom was surprised there was no accompanying call or text to explain why, but he was also relieved. As he held the Haven headset in his hands, he thought about whether it was a good idea to have told Amalia about the glitch. What if Atlasal figured out it wasn't just a typical system error? Could they trace the hack? Were they monitoring his sessions now?

As much as her tactics bothered him, he wished he had a way of contacting Nille. It wouldn't hurt to have her checking the network or cloud or whatever for any surveillance from Atlasal. Another client was supposed to have their first Haven session later in the day, so Dom decided to use the time meant for Jasmine to poke around in the system. No such thing as being too careful.

He locked his office door and put on the headset at his desk, activating the tutorial mode. The staff had used this when training with David. The mode allowed the user to roam around a randomized environment, testing out various exercises that a client might use. He wasn't sure what he was expecting to find. Without any hacking skills of his own, there wasn't anything he could do. After a few aimless minutes, he tore off the headset with a huff, then put his head down on the desk.

The knob jostled and forceful knocks rattled the door. "Yo, Dom, you alright in there?"

Louis' voice woke Dom up. He didn't realize he'd dozed off. Looking down at his watch, he saw it was the middle of his lunch break. He slunk his way over to the door. "Yeah, I'm good," he said, scratching his head as Louis looked at him sideways.

"You sure? You look like you had a rough weekend or something."

"Yeah, you could say that," Dom replied.

"Maybe some food will give you a boost," Louis said. "Wanna grab a bite?"

At the sandwich shop around the corner, Louis continued questioning. "For real, what's got you so down?"

"Nothing really," Dom said before biting into his turkey club sandwich. "Just some family stuff, but you know how that goes," he said with a shrug. It wasn't that much of a lie. "So, how are the Haven sessions going for you? Still think you're going to win the contest?"

Louis happily followed the change of subject to competition. "Man, I've got that contest on lock now that that overpriced gadget isn't crashing on me! I'm telling you, it's working magic with my clients. I've got this one six-year-old that would cry every session. Not like the good, you've-made-a-breakthrough cry, but more like the why-is-my-mom-forcing-me-to-talk-to-this-man cry. Once we finally got to use the headset, he was like a whole new kid. He breezes through the exercises and is actually excited to talk to me about what he learned. Same with this middle-aged guy I'm working with. His boss said he had to go to therapy to deal with his outbursts at work. The first few sessions, I got the brunt of that anger. Just complaining about his job, his boss, his wife, everything. I put those damn goggles on him and it turns out he can be a pretty chill guy. I just follow the program's lead and everything goes smoothly."

"Sounds like a big turnaround. This is the most highly I've heard you speak about Haven," Dom said.

"Hey, if it works, it works," Louis said. "How about your sessions?"

"Uh," he took a sip of his water. "I ran into a little hiccup myself, but I think Amalia let David know about it so it shouldn't be an issue. But it's seemed pretty help-ful so far."

"You better hope it's not an issue, because guess who's coming to our first leaderboard check-in?" Louis teased, eyebrow raised.

"Who?" Dom tried to sound intrigued.

"Our elusive CEO! Apparently, she's been doing a lot of travel since you started at New Horizons, on At-lasal's dime I assume, but my supervisor told me Stacy's making it a point to be here for the event."

Dom imagined the messages Nille had conjured up to make sure Stacy and Miranda were in the city at the same time. "Cool. Nice of her to show up for the company she runs."

"Right?" Louis laughed harder than Dom intended the quip to warrant. "Rich people problems, I guess."

Despite the satisfying lunch, Dom's stomach felt uneasy as he waited for his first afternoon client to ar-rive. It was a ten-year-old boy working on improving his impulse control. No reason for Atlasal to be suspicious about this session, right?

He watched his tablet closely throughout the young boy's VR session. Haven had created a fishing exercise for him. Dom took on the role of amateur marine biolo-gist, looking for glitches like strange features on the fish, or changes in the surrounding water that might signal the session was being monitored. As if he would be gift-ed a clue to let him know he was on Atlasal's watchlist.

By the time the session was over, his eyes stung from holding the tablet so close to his face.

Dom left the office that evening wondering again if he should bother coming back the next day. He couldn't continue having one paranoid session after another until Stacy and Miranda were in town. He wanted nothing more than to shut his eyes and forget about everything on the bus ride home, but when he got to the top step and looked down the aisle, a memorable set of thick locs caught his eye in the back row. A quick, two-finger salute sent Dom's way signaled that he'd have to seek out that relief later.

Sitting down next to Charles' large frame, Dom felt like a child. "So, you're the one spying on me now instead of Maurice?"

"No sir, spying ain't for me," he replied, displaying his grill with a fake grin. "I'm just being a guide today. Make sure you get where you need to be."

Dom sighed. "I'm assuming that's not home." He shook his head. "I really need to get a car."

Charles let out a sound Dom assumed was the closest thing to a laugh he would hear from him. "You and your cousin with that sarcasm."

Dom remembered his mom and Auntie Grace saying the same thing about them growing up. "Oh, I'm not joking. Being followed around and told where to go is pretty serious to me."

"This is better than the tactics your cousin used, right?"

Dom was admittedly glad to not be confronted by Charles alone on a dark street.

"We know you got a rough introduction to the group. There's still a lot more for you to learn though, so I'm bringing you to another spot of ours to start getting to know us in a different way."

There was no arguing with the decision, so Dom figured it would be useful to learn more about the people Maurice had spent the last five years with. "Since this is a re-introduction, how did you end up joining...the group?"

As more passengers got on the bus, Charles shook his head, signaling to put their conversation on hold. The forced silence in the name of secrecy made Dom think about Maurice. About how his cousin came to prefer being in the shadows of society. Purposefully removing himself from his family and community for the comfort of the unknown. By the time they got off at the next stop, Dom followed behind Charles with a renewed simmering anger at the mysterious organization that had taken his cousin from him.

Charles turned down a side street just past a church on the corner. Given that Dom was unconscious when entering and blindfolded when leaving the place he met The Village, he had no idea where this new spot was relative to the initial one.

Charles seemed to sense his confusion. "Like the maroons, we don't stay in one place too long."

"So, tell me. How did you join The Village?" Dom asked.

Charles' gait slowed. He whipped his head, tossing a loc behind his shoulder. "I was young when I first met Axel. Just out of high school."

A year younger than Maurice was when he met Axel, Dom thought. It seemed she had a type when it came to recruiting.

"I had recently joined the Marines," Charles continued. "I was out at lunch one day with some buddies, all of us in uniform. I used to get such a rush from putting it on. Funny how camouflage made us stand out amongst civilians. I went up to the counter to order and she just came up beside me, looked me dead in my eyes, and said, 'You know you're fighting the wrong war.'"

Dom looked down at the stylized brown and white camo pattern on Charles' pants.

Charles smirked, noticing this. "Other than looking cool, these patterns remind me of the world I walked away from. Although, I didn't really join the military for the fighting. Man, I was so young at the time, truthfully, I probably had more interest in finding out what evidence of aliens the government was hiding." Another awkward laugh before his face turned from amused to grim. "But then you find out what it's really all about. Money, resources worth money, land worth even more money. I think I was lost from the beginning. Looking for something bigger than myself to give me purpose. Axel was able to see that in me right away."

"That's not an uncommon reason for young people to join the military though, right?" Dom wondered how Axel decided who to approach with her pitch. Did she see a void or a vulnerability?

"You're right," Charles answered. "But why not be a part of something that builds rather than destroys? That's how Axel put it to me. The Village chooses helping over harming. Life over death. The maroon legacy of survival and spreading true freedom made the choice easy for me. Now, I'm not only fighting for something bigger than me, I'm fighting for something better than me." Charles came to a stop at the edge of a small plot of cultivated land.

"What's this?" Dom asked. Of course, he knew a farm when he saw one, but because he was such a city kid, he hadn't really thought about any being close to where he lived. It couldn't have been there before he left for grad school.

"It's ours is what it is," Charles said with pride. "Selling what we produce is one of the ways our hub covers its expenses."

Dom wondered what those expenses were.

They continued walking past a small raised, garden before Charles made a quick turn into a wooded area. Several yards in, he stopped and crouched down. Ruffling through some leaves, he picked out a lock and scrolled through a four-digit combination. Swinging up with the ease that came with his strength, a rectangular, wooden door opened to reveal steps leading underground.

What seemed to be a well-constructed tunnel stretched ahead of them. Charles and Dom used their cell phone lights to guide them forward. The tunnel only had a couple of turns in it and no branches, so getting lost was basically impossible. Still, Dom felt disoriented, the time on his phone giving him the only sense of how far they had walked. The minutes felt like hours in the cramped space. Finally, they reached a metal door.

"Here we are. Glad I don't have to tie you up this time."

CHAPTER
THIRTEEN

THE FEAR FROM TWO NIGHTS AGO CREPT BACK INTO Dom's chest as he entered the space. He wondered if this location was another place The Village brought unconscious recruits. The surroundings appeared to be that of a gutted basement, but of what building? Dom looked up, unable to decipher where in the city they might be after walking through the tunnel. Half the space was demarcated with false walls, creating a cluster of makeshift rooms.

"Like I said before, we have to be able to move quickly when necessary," Charles explained. "Just like the originators of The Village, mobility is a strength."

Dom looked around some more.

"Maurice isn't here." Nille peaked her head out from one of the constructed rooms off to Dom's left. "He's out with Axel getting supplies for the farm. Just me and Francis down here. Sorry." She gave a forced pout.

Charles put his hand on Dom's shoulder. "That's alright. Why don't you show Dom some of the other stuff you're working on while I go straighten things up upstairs."

Nille cupped her hand next to her mouth and loudly whispered, "That means take a nap. There's nothing to 'straighten up' up there." She playfully rolled her eyes as Charles walked off. "Come on, then. I can give you a peak at some things."

Dom followed her back through the makeshift hallways to a small room lit only by the light from the hallway. A mobile desk with Nille's multi-monitor setup was positioned in the corner. He reached for the string hanging from a light bulb in the center of the room, but Nille's hand on his forearm stopped him.

"Unh unh. Don't ruin the mood." She looked up at him. "Just kidding, but gotta protect these gems," she said, tapping the pool of pale skin surrounding her left eye. "Vitiligo doesn't just add to my beauty; it also makes my eyes sensitive to light."

"Oh, I didn't know."

"You didn't know I have vitiligo?"

"No, I meant—"

Nille's laugh broke through his stammering as she sat at the desk.

Quickly changing the subject, Dom said, "So, I heard that Stacy is coming to the first meeting regarding the Atlasal contest. Clever excuse to get her here with Miranda." He pulled a chair up next to Nille.

She nodded with sudden realization. "Oh, yeah, I saw the itinerary in her inbox. Wasn't me, though. She decided on the trip and the visit to New Horizons on her own, which sure took a heap of work off my plate. Now I just gotta coordinate the meetup and file exchange when they're here."

The center monitor flickered to life first, dimmed by a slim cover, followed by the others after Nille swiftly typed in a password. She clicked around, closing documents and moving files around before Dom could catch a glimpse of any. "Can't give away all the Village secrets just yet," she said, glancing over. "Not 'til you're one of us."

Although he'd been called a recruit, he had no desire to become a part of the group that had kept his cousin from him. "How did you join The Village?" Dom asked, curious to find a pattern in their recruitment.

"I'm guessing Charles told you his story," she said. "Pretty dramatic, huh? With me, I got into this because I wanted to. I was looking for a group like this. When you're someone with extracurricular computer skills, you tend to poke around in places you're not supposed to and usually find out information you didn't really want to know but know that everybody else should know. Ya know?"

"Makes sense. Government secrets and all," Dom said.

"Oh, everybody's got secrets. I was living in Oakland at the time. Lots of community organizing there, so I was connecting with people who shared the same general distrust of the institutions controlling us, only I knew the details to back up those suspicions. Long story short, one guy who could tell I was holding back on info took a risk and told me he was part of The Village. I was linked up with the hub out there for a while, and then someone told me the hub here in Selton City needed extra support, so I showed up." She clicked on an icon to open a program.

"Not much recruitment needed for you, it sounds like," Dom said.

"We're all willing participants in the end. No one is forced to join," Nille replied. "Here, I'll start you off with something basic. Take a look at this."

On the center screen, blue outlines created a 3D map of Selton City in the middle of a black space. The sculpture from Kendra's art show briefly flashed through Dom's mind.

"I'm not exactly sure what I'm going to do with this yet, but I've been running through different local government databases, some public, some not so much. Looking for patterns." Another click, and red dots populated the 3D map, most concentrated on the south side of the city.

"This one's got my wheels spinning," she continued. "Of course, you probably know most of the bogus fines the city collects comes from nitpicky violations that poor people are more likely to run into or just not be able to fully pay off. I'm thinking of a little Robin Hood maneuver to get some of those funds back. Here, I'll show you. You got any tickets?"

"I've never had a car," Dom said, leaving out the fact he'd ran a light or two when Kendra occasionally let him drive her car.

"Hmm, let's be sure of that. I'll just search your government name in this database over here…" She typed in D-O-M-I before Dom interrupted.

"No, not Dominic. My full name is Freedom, actually," he said looking away sheepishly.

"Oh, okay my brotha!" Nille said, holding up a Black Power fist.

"Don't act like you don't already know all my personal info." He continued avoiding her stare.

"Don't act like it's not still a dope ass name," she said, lightly tapping her fist on his shoulder. "Anyway, I need to figure out whether to play the long game and skim some funds from other places or just wipe the debts clean in one sweep."

Dom pushed away from the desk. "Damn, I'm sure Atlasal would love to have your technical skills on their team. Speaking of which, I wanted to ask you if I should be worried about them watching me more closely after the hack. They get all of our Haven data anyway, so do you think they picked up on anything?"

Nille looked over her glasses, raising an eyebrow. "Those tech bros? Please, they couldn't spot a hack, even the sloppy one I used, if their stock options depended on it. Erasing the video evidence was enough. You've got nothing to worry about."

A small bit of ease settled into Dom's body. "If I do notice anything suspicious going on with Haven, how do I notify you?"

"Wow, asking for my number already? Only official Village members get that."

"No, that's not what I meant," he said, standing up and moving behind his chair like it was a barrier. "And I feel like with me agreeing to steal Atlasal's secrets for you guys, I'm already pretty official, whether I want to be or not. Right?"

"No." Francis entered, startling Dom with his sharp answer. Even Nille straightened in her chair. "If you don't mind, Nille, it sounds like I need to give our guest a little more grounding in how things work around here." His request left no room for any other response.

"Sure thing, Francis." Nille turned back to her desk, continuing to fidget around with the database.

Francis walked away, not waiting to confirm that Dom was following. Dom chose to keep some distance as he trailed behind. They went to the other side of the basement, into a darkroom lined with developing photographs.

"So, how do people typically become official members?" Dom asked. "Seems like Charles was unexpectedly recruited while Nille was looking for something like this. And Maurice..." His jaw tightened, thinking about

Maurice's explanation for not coming back home. "After that initial contact—kidnapping in my case—what makes someone official?"

Francis glided amongst the hanging photos, checking their progress. "I'm glad everyone felt like sharing their origin stories, but I won't waste time with mine. It's all in our archive. If in some world you were ever allowed to join us, you could read all about it yourself. What I'll tell you now are the basics: initiation and naming."

All Dom could think about were the hazing rituals he heard so many college fraternities used.

"Recruits are vetted before they're approached," Francis explained. "Once we know a recruit wants to join for the right reasons and they've demonstrated their dedication, there is an initiation ceremony to recognize their transition into The Village."

"I thought there's no central leadership though," Dom said. "How do you know every hub has the same qualifications to join and does the same initiation?"

Francis huffed. "I forgot how many questions you ask. You're right, there's no oversight on how recruitment happens, but The Village was founded on strong principles. These principles are our root, so no matter how far we spread we are still anchored in them."

"And what if someone doesn't want to become a member?" Dom asked.

"As Maurice told you, not many people would believe the story, so we don't worry about people turning our offer down. It's only happened a handful of times with this hub. Besides, just like our maroon ancestors, discovery is not our destruction; we have many means of escape." He moved back to the next row of photos.

"And before you ask," Francis continued, "our naming process is connected to our history. Every new member of The Village chooses a new name that reflects their commitment. Some are the actual names or derivatives of maroons; all are those of fighters. My name comes from Francois Makandal, the Haitian maroon leader, burned at the stake for his resistance. 'Nille' is a shortened form referencing Petronille Dwine, a St. Lucian maroon, also killed for her actions. 'Charles' mirrors Charles Deslondes, who led a revolt of the enslaved in Louisiana. Again, he was killed as a result. And 'Axel' takes her name from Axeline Elizabeth Salomon, one of the Danish, now United States, Virgin Islands' Fireburn Queens who led a labor revolt."

Dom's mouth hung open as he took in all the history. These were names he had never heard. He instinctively knew this was intentional. These were heroes who were never placed on the pedestals of history where they could be easily discovered.

"What about Maurice?" Dom asked.

Francis rolled his eyes to the ceiling. "He got lucky. Maurice Bishop was the briefly realized revolutionary leader of Grenada, killed in a coup. Your cousin was too stubborn to choose a name other than his own."

Another unknown name. Dom wondered how much this version of Maurice he'd rediscovered resembled the historical figure of the same name.

The last photo in the back row was the only one fully developed. As Dom came to stand next to Francis, he shouted. "Hey!" The pride and wonder he was feeling from the brief history lesson shifted to disgust as he recognized himself in the photo hanging before him, gagged and blindfolded. "Why do you have this?" The fact that his own cousin had put him in that position made the image even harder to see.

"Relax," Francis said, sternly. "As Village archivist, it's my job to document. And unlike most governments and institutions, I think it's important to remember our mistakes. This is evidence of poor decision making that we will keep in our records in order to avoid ever mistreating someone like this again."

The explanation didn't stop a queasy feeling from developing in Dom's stomach. It bubbled up into rage. "No! This isn't right. Taking Maurice away from me and my family was a pretty big mistake, don't you think? You mistreated us by thinking you could do better for him than we could. Did The Village keep records and take any lessons from that?"

He ripped down a line of photos as he stormed out of the darkroom.

"Fine, leave," Francis said. "Leave us and Maurice. Go back to that job to save the world with those video game goggles."

The mocking tone of the last comment matched Kendra's in a way that almost made Dom snap completely. Luckily, Charles came down in time to intervene, leading Dom out of the hideout and away from any rash decisions.

CHAPTER

FOURTEEN

D OM'S PHONE BUZZED IN HIS POCKET FOR THE third time in five minutes. He apologized to Amalia, letting her know it was Ms. Henry calling him. He placed the ringer on silent to focus on their supervision session, but a text popped up right before he placed the phone back in his pocket.

Jasmine ran away again! Call Me

"Shit."

"Something we need to discuss?" Amalia asked.

"Jasmine's missing again." His body felt hot. He couldn't stop tapping his foot.

"Oh, no. I hope she comes back quickly like last time. Missing another session won't be good." She seemed to be talking more to herself than to Dom.

If Jasmine had come to their previous session, maybe he could have helped to prevent whatever made her run away this time.

"Take a breath," Amalia said, noticing Dom's continued fidgeting. "There's not much you can do right now."

"I gotta do something," Dom said. "There's something out there she's looking for. Her mom and her home seem too normal for her to be escaping anything, so it's gotta be the other way around. Whatever she's seeking, it's not safe out there."

"You're right. That's why we have the police," Amalia said. "You've done great in your sessions with her so far, but we can't solve every problem as therapists."

Dom had never been this annoyed with Amalia. She didn't sound like the person he'd met a month ago. "You know what it's like when Black girls go missing."

Amalia twisted her mouth in thought, nodding slowly. She seemed to be mulling over different responses.

"This is now twice within a few weeks," Dom continued. "Are the police really going to care? Do you?"

"Dom!" Amalia straightened up. "Of course I care. This is a complicated issue. I'm more than aware of how our lives are valued and how that influences how resources are used for our benefit. What I'm speaking to is your role as Jasmine's therapist. I don't need you crossing any lines by getting too involved in this. You can talk to Ms. Henry to support her and help create a plan for how she will manage emotionally while the authorities look for Jasmine and what she will do to ensure Jasmine's safety upon return. But nothing else."

An old frustration took hold. Amalia's words were similar to the way authorities had spoken to Dom's parents after Maurice disappeared. They tried to make it seem like they understood. Like they had everything under control. The family just needed to let the professionals do their job. Before months could even become a year, they were told to accept the professionals' conclusion and begin playing the role of bereaved family assigned to them by the facts of the case.

"No, I gotta find her," he mumbled. He got up, turning to leave.

"Dom, you're not about to go looking for her," Amalia demanded, also standing. "You have other clients coming in today." She looked on incredulously as Dom walked out of her office.

Outside of New Horizons, Dom paid for a rental bike at a nearby rack. He didn't pause to think about the consequences of walking out of work. The summer air dragged its humidity around him as he pedaled toward Jackson Park. He had no reason to believe Jasmine would have gone to the same place as last time. Surely, Ms. Henry had looked there already, but he had nowhere else to start.

Jackson was one of the larger parks in the city. Dom pulled up to its edge, near a statue of its namesake; some explorer from centuries ago, pointing off into the distance as if mocking the difficulty of finding Jasmine. Dom wheeled his way down a path, passing by playground equipment and sets of benches. His head darted back and forth, analyzing each face he saw. One figure wearing a hoodie in the sticky heat caught his eye, but it was false hope. Just a man dressed inappropriately for the weather. This area of the park felt too exposed. Not somewhere to stay missing.

He followed a trail that went into the woods lining the city's north side. It was a popular trail, with hikers and bikers typically dotting its expansive length. Right now, it was nearly empty. Dom continued forward for a few minutes before stopping and resting the bike against a tree. It didn't make sense to keep looking in one area. He was already tired, but couldn't give up.

He flashed back to some of the search efforts he participated in when Maurice went missing. It always felt like his cousin could be right around a corner or an obvious clue would turn up within minutes of starting a search sweep. If only he had known how close Maurice really was.

Leaving Jackson Park behind, Dom decided to head east, in the direction of Jasmine's home. After several blocks, a sliver of his therapist training was able to breakthrough the frenzy. Yes, he was riding around the city looking for his client, but going to her house—the one she ran away from—was perhaps one boundary crossing too far. A quick detour led him to her school instead, not thinking that it was summertime and it was another place she was trying to avoid. Two loops around the building confirmed there was nothing to find there.

Lost on where to go next, he headed south toward his apartment. Along the way, he checked inside a random clothing store, peaked into an ice cream shop, and even stopped at a church just in case Jasmine thought no one would look there. Unwilling to accept defeat, he reluctantly admitted he was out of ideas.

Numb in so many ways, he felt carried along by some force as the streets slid by him in a blur. When the fog in his mind parted, he realized he had biked past his apartment all the way to his parents' house.

As he let the bike drop in the front yard, the exhaustion of traversing nearly half the city finally hit him. Hands on his knees, he heaved deep breaths that felt desperate for more than just air. Scraping his feet through the grass, he knocked on the front door, too worn out to fumble for his key.

"Dom!" his mom looked at him with wide eyes. "Are you okay?" She pulled him inside, guiding him to the living room. "Sit. Let me get you some water."

His dad turned from the TV. "You look beat. Did you walk over here in all this heat?"

The words sounded muffled and like they stopped a few inches from Dom's head. His mom placed a glass of water in his hand. The cold sip brought back some clarity to his surroundings.

"What's going on?" his dad asked.

"Work," Dom said, after a pause.

"Okay? I thought you were enjoying your job," his mom said.

"Yeah, and what's it got to do with you looking like this?" his dad added.

Looking out the living room window, Dom noticed the sun had crept closer to the horizon. The approaching night made him more scared for Jasmine. He dropped his head into his hand. "It's...it's one of my clients."

"Oh, no." His dad put a hand on Dom's shoulder.

"I knew this career would be too much," his mom said. "Kids are hurting themselves more and more nowadays."

Dom shook his head. "No, it's not that. She's...she's gone missing again. I'm worried she's not going to come back this time. I left work to look for her—" he broke; tears flowed. He couldn't remember the last time he cried in front of his parents.

For the first time in years, their own pain was not hidden behind forced conclusions. The double embrace they gave Dom felt like an acknowledgement that there was something incomplete in their family dynamic.

"We get it," his mom said through sobs of her own.

"We know it still hurts," his dad said.

A jolt of frustration rattled Dom's body as he fought to keep in the secret of his recent discovery. Somehow, he'd only become more isolated since reuniting with the missing piece he'd hoped to find for so long.

After a couple gulps of water, he started to feel more regulated. He also started thinking more clearly.

"You think I'll get in trouble for walking out of work like that?"

His parents looked at each other.

"I don't know about that," his dad said, "but you should stay here this weekend to try to get your mind off things. Worry about work when it's time to go back."

After dinner, Dom trudged upstairs, the day's events forcing an early bedtime on him. The office door was partially open when he reached the top step. Maurice's graduation photo stared back at him as his phone buzzed in his pocket. It was a message from an unknown number.

Meet at Parkside Library tomorrow. 10am.

CHAPTER

FIFTEEN

THE LIBRARY WAS SPARSE WHEN DOM ARRIVED.

He walked up and down the rows of books, looking for whoever he was supposed to meet with. He figured it was someone from The Village who texted him, but he didn't know who would want to meet up so close to his home and in a place where they couldn't talk openly.

Rounding the corner of the reference section, he spotted Francis sitting at a table with books piled high. His hands were like birds flitting from branch to branch as he splayed multiple books before him, flipping through pages and taking notes. Once Dom got closer, he saw someone else slouched in the chair next to Francis. All Dom could see under the person's low cap brim was a short goatee.

Dom knocked once on the table, giving a silent nod as Francis looked up from the books in front of him. Dom's eyes darted over at the unknown person.

"Would you sit down already?" Francis said in a quiet tone. "You're late." He looked over at the man next to him. "Why couldn't you do this on your own?"

The man looked over and then up at Dom, green eyes piercing. He winked and motioned at the chair across from him. Through the colored contacts, goatee, and layer of makeup, Dom gleaned the general shape of Maurice's face.

"So, this is what you do now? What you've been doing all this time?" Dom asked. "Playing dress-up to hide from the people who care about you."

"Not right now, Dom," Maurice said, sitting up. "Like Francis said, we don't have much time."

"My bad, I didn't keep my eye on the clock since I knew it was a quick walk over from *Mom and Dad's house*." He waved an arm in the direction of the house while glaring at Maurice. He saw Maurice gulp and shift his green eyes away briefly. Dom pulled his chair back and slammed it down with a reverberating thud.

"I need to make sure we're still on the same page as far as the Atlasal plan," Maurice said, keeping his voice low as someone walked through their area. "I heard when you were at our place earlier this week, an issue came up."

"Oh, the huge photo of my kidnapping? That issue?" Dom asked. "You guys sure have a way with downplaying your actions."

"Look," Maurice lowered his voice even more. "I didn't have us come here to argue more. I need to know that you're still okay with the plan."

"Okay with it?" Dom folded his arms. "I don't feel like I really have a choice, but honestly, I have other things on my mind right now."

"Distractions aren't going to help," Maurice said.

"One of my clients has gone missing for a second time," Dom explained. "I know disappearing isn't a big deal to you, but I think it's valid for me to be concerned."

Maurice looked down at the table. "I get it," he nodded slowly, still looking down. "I understand more than you think I do."

"No, you don't," Dom said.

Maurice sighed, rubbing his hands on his lap.

"The Village tracked me pretty easily, so can't you guys help find my client?" Dom asked.

"No, we don't have the ability to do that," Maurice said.

"What are you going to do when she's found anyway?" Francis peeked over his stack of books. "All that therapy and she's still running away. You think more of it will help her?"

Dom sent the stack of books careening over with a single push, removing any obstacle between them. "What's that supposed to mean? You're telling me therapy doesn't work? I thought The Village was all about healing."

"Yes, real healing," Francis answered.

Maurice reacted to the biting tone, placing his forehead in his hands.

"If you stop getting mad and just listen, you could learn a thing or two about how to be a true healer," Francis continued.

"What is it you think you can teach me?" Dom asked.

"For starters, not to be so arrogant," Francis quipped. Before Dom could react, Francis continued. "More importantly, you need to realize your clients don't exist." He put a finger up to stop any interruption. "What I mean is, the population of people you're working with doesn't exist in the eyes of this society."

Dom knew the people in his part of the city were overlooked, but he never thought of it the way Francis was describing.

"Think about it as a kind of social death," Francis explained. "Sure, the people are physically alive, but you wouldn't be convinced of it based on how they're treated by society. You can't resurrect someone from social death with therapy. With the way you were trained, at best you might only help them adjust to their condition."

The last statement rattled Dom. How could the practice he'd chosen to help his community be cast aside so easily as being ultimately worthless?

"But if you make them aware of this state of non-being, they can begin to develop the capacity to liberate themselves." Francis looked deep into Dom's eyes, searching for a sign that anything he was saying was sinking in.

"I'm not going to give up on Jasmine. Or anyone else that I know I have the skills to help just because you don't like therapy," Dom said.

"It's not about what I like. It's about what I know," Francis rebutted. "It doesn't take mountains of debt and specialized training to learn your own history. Your school didn't teach you anything about the practices our ancestors used that were banned or beat out of them in favor of Western medicine and Christianity."

"Ancestral practices? I don't believe in all that magic stuff you're talking about. Just because it's ancient doesn't mean it's right," Dom said.

Francis sat back, looking off to the side in disbelief. "The words of the master. If I closed my eyes, I'd think I was talking to an old white man."

"Francis!" Maurice nudged him.

"No! This boy is too much. Come with me," Francis got up, motioning for Dom to follow.

With a huff, Dom complied, mostly so he didn't have to keep looking at his cousin in his ridiculous disguise.

Maurice pulled his hat lower as he was left alone.

Francis walked briskly across the library, passing aisle after aisle until he reached his destination. He reached up, standing on his toes for a half second to grab a book. He placed the thick, heavy hardcover in Dom's hands.

"There aren't too many texts that explore the early Caribbean like this one," Francis explained.

On the cover, rather than the tropical landscape seen in tourist advertisements, various artifacts unfamiliar to Dom were displayed. He shrugged. "Like I said, all the dolls, potions, chants, and what not aren't for me. None of the parents of the kids I work with would let me use that stuff, anyway."

Francis shook his head. "There's way more to the healing systems of the diaspora than you're aware of, clearly, but you're still missing the point. I'm not telling you about this history to show you techniques that are better than the ones you use now. Rather, what's important is that what you've been taught about how to help people completely ignores this history. People all over the world engaged in healing practices way before Freud had anything to say on the matter. You would benefit from expanding your knowledge base."

"Yes, I know Europeans didn't invent healing. But I'm not hurting anyone with the therapy I'm providing," Dom said.

"You sure about that?" Francis led him to another aisle. He handed Dom another book, pointing to the words "Liberation Psychology" in its subtitle. "These two words come up in your classes?"

Dom thought about it. "If it was in a textbook, I don't remember, but I know it was never discussed."

"Mhm. As I thought." Francis leaned on the bookshelf. "The therapy you were trained to do is all about the individual. Concepts like liberation psychology understand that there are structures that shape people's lived realities, especially oppressed people. When a person stuck in the gears of interlocking systems reaches out for help and all they get is a strategy for changing their thoughts, don't you think that could hurt?"

What Francis said made sense. There wasn't anything about his clients that made him think there was something inherently "wrong" with them. As much as Jasmine's actions frustrated him, he knew the reason behind them didn't start and stop with brain chemistry. Helping Parkside was always about responding to the conditions people were living in. Why wasn't he trained in this framework of liberation?

"Guys, what's taking you so long?" Maurice darted around a corner alongside them.

"Just trying to open your cousin's mind," Francis answered.

"I didn't know I'd be getting homework today," Dom said, grasping both books in his hand.

"Well, I have another assignment for you before you leave," Maurice said.

He led Dom upstairs, quickly scurrying behind a bookshelf. "Check the study room over there," he said, pointing with his thumb.

Dom peaked around the bookshelf at one of the glass-walled study rooms. The two-person room had a single occupant. Her back was turned to the glass, but the curly hair pulled back into a puff and the design on her pink jacket gave Kendra away. Dom looked back at Maurice, shrugging and raising his palms.

"Go talk to her. You need to," Maurice said. "Like I said before, distractions aren't going to help. You may think you're successfully ignoring the feud going on between the two of you, but it will get in the way eventually."

"Wait, how do you know we're not cool?" Dom raised his voice. "You have me bugged or something?"

"Shh!" Maurice looked back and forth with his finger to his mouth. Something in this motion reminded Dom of when they played hide-and-go-seek as kids. Despite his current frustration with Maurice, he had to fight back a smile.

"Not exactly. Let's just say I had eyes on the scene at the art gallery," Maurice continued. "I needed to in order to make sure we...crossed paths that night. After seeing how y'all went at each other, I know you're still feeling something. That's your best friend."

"She was your friend, too," Dom said. Emotions spun through his head. The creepy surveillance he'd been under for who knew how long, the continued distancing of Maurice from his past, and the thought of what to say to Kendra. He didn't have an apology. She was the one who needed to apologize, but he doubted she was ready for that, either.

Dom knocked gently on the glass of the study room. When Kendra turned and her eyes met his, she quickly swung back around, shaking her head.

He knocked again. "Please. We need to talk."

Kendra's shoulders rose and dropped with a sigh. She reached behind her and opened the door without looking. As Dom entered, he saw Kendra was working on a sketch of a tiger, crouching in tall grass.

"Nice. Working on a new gallery show?" he asked.

"Nope. I was supposed to give a neighbor's kid a drawing lesson, but she didn't show." She kept her eyes on the paper.

"Well, since I'm here, you could teach me something," Dom said. Kendra's pencil continued moving, uninterrupted. "I'll pay for the lesson. You got a friend discount?"

Kendra dropped her pencil, sitting back with crossed arms. "Why are you here? Like, not just talking to me, but why are you even at the library? I didn't think you spent your weekends here."

Dom looked over her shoulder at the bookshelf he had walked over from. It was a strange feeling knowing that the person at the core of their argument at the gallery show was just that close. "There was just a...a book I wanted to try. Liberation Psychology."

"Sounds...profound," Kendra said.

"Gotta stay mission-ready. You know, golden child shit." He raised his eyebrows.

Kendra started to collect her papers together.

"Wait! Sorry, I didn't come here to be a jerk." Dom looked up at the ceiling, gathering his thoughts. "As much as I think I was justified, I guess I want to try to understand."

"I said what I had to say at my show," Kendra stated plainly. "There's nothing more to understand."

"I just," Dom hesitated. "You know I didn't run away. Going to California wasn't about escaping. It was about building the skills I needed and bringing them back to Parkside."

"Those skills were something you became obsessed with after Maurice went missing," Kendra said. "From the outside looking in, the way this desire weighed on you was obvious. You really wanted to be the one to save him. Like you could have changed the course of his life. And you're still trying to save him through these kids you work with."

Her analysis stung, but he couldn't deny it. Even with Maurice's return, it was his disappearance that drove Dom's frantic need to find Jasmine. He chose not to tell Kendra about Jasmine, because he didn't need this to turn into an "I told you so" conversation.

"Is it wrong to have wanted to save him?" Dom asked.

"What would that even look like? If he did come back and you did get the chance to help him, would that change anything about why he left in the first place?"

His shoulders dipped. Kendra had been the only person he could really talk to about his theory that Maurice was still alive. She had listened without judging, even agreeing with the possibility, which made her question just now that much harder to answer. What could he do now? According to Maurice, there was apparently nothing to change. Dom was promised more answers about the past five years. It had been a whirlwind of a week, but he couldn't wait any longer.

"Sorry, I know talking about him is hard," Kendra said, idly picking at her nails.

"No, it's okay. It'd be worse if we stopped talking about him." Dom felt like his lungs would collapse under the pressure of holding in the truth about Maurice. He jolted up out of his seat. "Thanks for talking. I know we didn't clear everything up, but just know that I hear you." He paused at the door. "Oh, and your sculpture did at least look pretty dope."

The corner of her mouth tilted up. "Thanks, I guess."

Dom returned to the bookshelf, but Maurice was gone.

AUGUST

CHAPTER

SIXTEEN

Weeks passed by with radio silence from The Village.

It was kind of nice not to have them on his back, but each day was another day without Maurice.

Dom listened to his call go straight to the full voicemail box again; he'd lost count of how many times he had tried calling Ms. Henry. He couldn't hold it against her for not answering. He knew all too well the emotions she was likely going through right now. Wondering. Hoping.

Sitting out front of a café, he turned his attention back to the library books. He initially started reading them to try to challenge Francis' perspective, but found that he was picking up lessons that were too applicable to ignore.

He read the details of Eighteenth and Nineteenth century laws passed in various Caribbean colonies, outlawing voodoo, obeah, and similar healing and religious practices out of fear. He contemplated how the practices he learned in grad school were sanctioned. What was it that made them acceptable over other approaches to healing? Not only was his therapeutic approach shaped by exclusionary processes like this, these biased approaches now informed programs like Haven for it to create virtual environments and activities. The new tech perpetuated an old cycle.

He was also beginning to admit to himself that maybe his connection to his clients wasn't as strong as he thought. Sure, he came from the same place as them and knew the environment they were growing up in, but he didn't really use that knowledge in his sessions. In order to be truly liberatory, he had to bring the structures shaping his clients into his work. The Haven headset was feeling more and more like a barrier, blocking out their surroundings rather than addressing the influence of them.

These thoughts stayed with him the next morning as he got ready for Stacy Connors' visit to New Horizons. On his way into the office, Dom saw a black Mercedes sedan parked in front of the building. He'd never seen a car that nice parked on their street. A burly man leaned on the hood, straining the sleeves of his dark blazer as he flicked away long strands of dirty blonde hair that didn't quite make it into his bun. Their eyes briefly met as the man put a cigarette to his mouth with a faded tattoo-covered hand. Dom quickened his steps inside.

The large conference room was full of energy. Every employee packed the space, creating a buzz of excited conversation. Louis was beaming as Dom sat next to him.

"You ready?" Louis rubbed his hands together, unable to sit still.

Dom shrugged. "I guess. It's just the first leaderboard check-in, so not sure why you're so pumped."

"Booo!" Louis shook his thumb downward. "Keep your rain cloud over there," he teased. "Having the big boss see that I'm crushing y'all this early on is a big deal."

Dom hadn't been thinking much about the competition. He didn't know how the missed sessions with Jasmine would factor in, but given why they were missed he really didn't care. As for his other clients, he knew they were doing well without Haven's confirmation.

"Plus," Louis continued, "someone posted a pic on social media that looked like Miranda Webb checking into a hotel in Selton City last night. Seems like we could have a surprise guest on our hands."

"Yeah, maybe." At least there was some sort of confirmation that Nille's plan was going accordingly so far.

Amalia entered, standing in front of the group to call them to attention. Things had been tense since he ran out of work to look for Jasmine. Amalia had graciously covered for him that day, letting his other clients know he had suddenly fallen ill, but ever since, her demeanor toward him was cold.

"Okay, everyone. Today's the big day!" she announced, smiling from ear to ear. She looked to her left, waving someone to her while mouthing, *"come on."* "I know a lot of you haven't met Stacy yet. She's been a busy woman, traveling around and spreading the word about the great work being done at New Horizons. But, she made sure not to miss this special day."

Stacy walked out, her red ponytail bobbing with each step. She waved at her employees like a celebrity waves at fans. Her pristine white suit signaled what she must rake in as head of the company. As she approached Amalia, Dom saw the slightest movement in Amalia's torso that looked as if she would have taken a bow if she didn't catch herself. Something unspoken passed between her and Stacy as the CEO placed a light hand on her elbow.

"Thanks so much, Amalia!" The red lipstick outlining Stacy's smile matched the blouse underneath her suit. Amalia took a few awkward steps to the side. "I'm so glad to be here with you all, especially the new faces we've added since I've been out. You're all so important in helping us move this Atlasal initiative forward. With you, New Horizons is blazing a new path." Her eyes moved quickly from face to face, the slight attention making each person straighten their posture in succession.

Dom felt like he was listening to the introductory video from his first day again. It seemed like sales pitch was Stacy's default mode.

"I wouldn't have chosen to be away from the office for so long if I didn't believe strongly in all the great work the Haven program is going to help us do. I've been talking to anyone with ears about what we've got going on here. Even though I've partnered up with the world's greatest saleswoman in Miranda Webb, people still need to see the data." Her lips pressed into a straight line, her focus seeming to drift for a split second. She blinked rapidly out of the brief hitch, wiping at the corners of her mouth before continuing.

"Which is why today is so important. I can't wait to see the progress that's been made in your sessions using Haven, and to reveal who's in the top spot and a step closer to having a sit down with Miranda."

Louis nodded his head confidently. "Here we go," he said to Dom.

"Alright, let's do this," Amalia stepped back up front, tablet in hand. "As you all know, symptom reduction is the primary measure of progress that's been tracked. So far, you've received weekly red, yellow, or green color-coded indicators of this progress, but today we'll be showing specific data points. This will be the weekly data you receive from this point forward for the remainder of the contest. So, without further delay..." She tapped on the tablet a few times.

"In third place..."

Louis clapped along with everyone else, happy his name wasn't announced yet.

"And in second is..."

"Sorry, bro, coulda been you," Louis said, nudging Dom.

"At the top of the leaderboard, this person had a slow start, but quickly got to it with implementing Haven. We'll see if he can keep it up. Give it up for Louis!"

Dom couldn't fight returning a genuine smile as Louis shot up from his seat. Louis dapped him up before going to the front of the room to shake Amalia's and Stacy's hands.

"Wow, great job, Louis!" Stacy sounded like she was congratulating a child for finishing his veggies. She angled her head, staring at him, one eye slightly squinting. "So, we don't have any prize for this stage of the contest, but if you have anything you want to say, any tips for everybody, go ahead."

Louis held his head high, looking across his co-workers. "As someone that wasn't so sure about using Haven at first, all I can say is to trust the program. Learning how it works and seeing how much my clients like using it has opened my eyes."

Dom tuned out the rest of Louis' infomercial. The time when he had a similar excitement about Haven felt distant.

At the end of the meeting, Louis began chatting up Stacy off to the side. Dom planned to finish up notes in his office, but as he tried to walk by, Louis pulled him into their conversation.

"Dom here was stoked about Haven from the start." Louis clapped him on the back. "We were supposed to be battling it out for the top spot in the contest, but I'm not sure what happened."

Dom glared at him for ignoring what he knew happened with Jasmine and for talking like that about him to their CEO.

"There's plenty of time to get back on track. I'm sure Amalia will be expecting as much," Stacy said, almost more to herself than Dom.

"Of course," Dom said, forcing a smile. "I'll be putting all my focus into improving. Excuse me, but I have some notes to complete."

Louis' sucking up to Stacy continued to bug him throughout the rest of the day. He left work a few minutes early to avoid having to talk to him about the contest anymore. As he walked outside, a phone call from an unknown number buzzed his pocket. He answered quickly.

"Nope, turn around. No bus today, cuz," Maurice's voice came through with a hint of mischief. "I'm parked at the other end of the block. Hurry, we have a reservation to make."

CHAPTER
SEVENTEEN

THE MITCHELL HAD A GROWING CROWD WAITING outside. Even on a Monday night, the city's only three-star restaurant maintained a packed guest list along with hopeful diners optimistically waiting for someone to miss a reservation.

Partway down the block and across the street, Dom and Maurice found a spot with a perfect view of the entrance, watching intently from a dark blue sedan.

"I don't get why we have to do a stake out when Nille has everything so meticulously planned," Dom said.

"I wouldn't consider it a stake out," Maurice explained. "We're just making sure everything goes smoothly. You and I keep watch out here while Nille and Axel stay close to the VIPs inside."

"Hmph, lucky." Dom plopped his head back on the headrest.

"You don't even eat fancy food like that," Maurice quipped.

"How would you know?"

Maurice huffed. "When Stacy and Miranda arrive, we'll notify Nille and Axel. They'll keep an eye on the pair to see that the USB handoff is made. If any of us sees anything fishy, we'll be in communication the whole time." He held his phone up, wiggling it back and forth.

"Sounds exciting. Now that I know we'll just be sitting here for the next few hours, I definitely would have asked to pick something up to eat," Dom grumbled.

"You'll be fine. Just focus on something else." His tone reminded Dom about when his dad would get annoyed with them and tell them to stop complaining. "Looks like it's go-time anyway." Maurice pointed past Dom.

On the opposite sidewalk, Axel and Nille strolled side by side in complementary simple black dresses. Axel was without her customary headwrap, sporting braids that swept across her shoulders and back; Nille's sleeveless dress revealed a colorful tattoo on her upper left arm.

Maurice put his phone on speaker, placing it in the cup holder. "Duck one and Duck two, this is Goose. Copy?"

Dom jerked slightly hearing the attempted humor. He saw Nille put a finger to her ear. "For someone that loves disguises, you're terrible with code names. Let's keep things normal and stick to the plan, okay?"

"Well, according to the plan, you two are running eight minutes late," Maurice replied.

As Axel and Nille approached The Mitchell's entrance, the man at the door put a hand out to stop them. A black Mercedes pulled up in front of the restaurant. Out of the driver's seat stepped the man with the bun Dom had seen earlier outside of New Horizons. He walked around the front of the car and opened the back passenger door.

"Hey, that guy was outside my office today," Dom said. "Must be Stacy's driver. Sure is nice to be CEO."

"It looks like we're right on time," Axel's voice came through reassuredly.

Out of the backseat, Stacy stood, her hair freely flowing over a fancy gown. She seemed to size up the crowd before giving room for the next person to exit.

Miranda Webb stepped out of the car with a helping hand from the driver. She walked directly behind Stacy, who led the way into the restaurant. People turned to each other with dazzled faces, several stealing a photo of Miranda as she walked by.

"Oh, to be a famous capitalist," Nille snarked. The man standing in their way moved aside, allowing her and Axel to enter. A few minutes of silence passed.

"They're at a table in the corner," Axel explained. "They've caused quite a buzz. We were able to request a different table to get a better line of sight."

"Alright then, nothing to note out here," Maurice replied. "Bun-dude took off and people are still losing it over Miranda."

"Bun-dude? Again with the code names," Nille groaned.

"Not a code name. Just a descriptor," Maurice responded.

Dom interrupted. "We'll let you know if we see anything important. Otherwise, we're listening'" He hit "mute" on Maurice's phone. The way Maurice seemed to so easily be lighthearted with his Village counterparts bugged him.

"I've never appreciated Freedom more," Nille said, amusement in her voice.

Dom shook his head.

"Been a while since I heard one of those puns," Maurice said. He sat back and closed his eyes, sliding his hat back so the brim pointed up at the middle of his head. "What did Uncle Abe used to say? Free them all, Freedom—"

"It's been a while since you've heard a lot of things," Dom interjected.

"Woah. Okay, okay." Maurice put his hands up. "Is it time to have that talk? We'll be sitting here for a while."

"Oh, you think it might be time?" Dom sat forward. "I don't know what's got you so lively tonight, joking around and all, but do you realize you still haven't explained anything to me? The five years. Your loyalty to The Village. Abandoning our family. None of it!"

Frustration built up as he watched Maurice sigh in response. There was nothing disguising Maurice's face tonight, no barrier to hide behind.

"Like I said the night I...introduced you to The Village, I had my reasons for not coming back." He opened his mouth to continue, but was interrupted again.

"We're getting seated now," Nille said, her words echoing in the cup holder. "They've got their entrees already. Speedy service for the special guests, I guess."

"Copy," Maurice responded before putting the phone back on mute. "I appreciate everything you, Uncle Abe, and Aunt Melanie did for me," he continued. "But it didn't change the fact that my mom was gone. Every day was just another reminder that I would never see her again. Hear her voice. Eat her food."

Dom recalled when his mom first got the news of her sister's death. She crumbled in on herself, like paper curling up as flames reduced it to ash. Knowing her sister had been sick did not lessen the devastation of losing her.

"I saw how it affected you," Dom said, his voice getting shaky. "How did leaving change any of that?"

"One of the most important things I learned from The Village is that the maroons found freedom in their flight. They established something new. Home is where you're free. And I wasn't feeling that in Parkside. The distance from the pain helped me," Maurice explained.

"Breaking out of the pattern of grief for a bit. Also, when I first met Axel, she filled in some blanks for me. There's so much that we don't get told."

He shifted to look directly at Dom. "Back when our parents were kids, there was this chemical processing facility near Parkside. The city never agreed to do any official studies, but many community members believed the kids who grew up in that area were affected physically and mentally, some worse than others. Axel said earlier Village members were part of the activist movement to get the facility shut down, but she suspected my mom was one of the unfortunate victims of an overlooked, forgotten problem. When I heard that story, immediately, it was like the sun broke through the clouds for the first time in years. I finally had some answers."

Dom had never heard about this chemical plant. Auntie Grace was laid to rest with no official diagnosis, and the shift in responsibility to care for Maurice kept anyone in the family from asking questions for much longer after.

"I guess I can understand needing time away from a place that holds so much pain. But that story was enough for you, even without knowing for sure it was related to your mom's death?" Dom asked. "And it convinced you to follow Axel?"

"I didn't need complete certainty about Mom's cause of death," Maurice explained. "Even if the chemical plant wasn't the actual cause, knowing that something was done in response to the community's needs changed something in me. What happens to you individually can be acted on collectively. That's what The Village is about."

The conviction in his words struck Dom.

"Okay, it looks like Webb is searching through her purse for something," Nille said softly, almost like she knew something profound had just been said in the car. "False alarm, just hand sanitizer...Pass along that USB so we can find out what else your hands are dirty with."

Maurice raised a quizzical eyebrow, but Dom was not ready to engage in any banter.

"So, that was it. The Village's convincing message kept you in their grip from then on." Dom rested his head on the window, staring off into the night.

"I was never 'in their grip,' geez," Maurice said. "Even though I was interested in The Village, Axel wasn't sure how I could contribute to them in my condition at the time. The occasional pills I took were still strong enough to do damage and I was just generally aimless. So, she sent me to a Village facility way up north, to help straighten me out."

"Like rehab?" Dom asked.

"Yes and no," Maurice answered. "The facility's public-facing identity shifts from time to time, but The Village has been operating it for their own purposes for decades. Healing, training, planning; lots of things go on there, but once I was good, I came back to Selton."

"And stayed in the shadows," Dom said.

"Not the whole time. I went out to California a couple times to see you," Maurice said.

Heat rose up Dom's body, but he bit the inside of his cheek to keep from blowing up. "At this point, nothing should surprise me, but spying on me while I was pursuing the education that was motivated by your disappearance is...is...I needed you, Maurice!"

"Dom, I—"

"Transfer confirmed!" Nille blared from the cup holder. "The wine's got them talking a little louder. Something about keep it...off this...at my place?"

"A safe in her office," Axel relayed. "The USB is going to be stored in a safe in Stacy's office."

Dom and Maurice gave awkward nods to each other. "Got it," Maurice responded.

"They just asked for the check, too," Axel said. "You guys keep an eye out as they leave."

"Yeah, we're gonna finish this amazing food. Why don't you save us some time and just chase their car down, put 'em in a tailspin, and then snatch the USB before the cops show up," Nille chuckled.

"We'll pass," Dom replied. He and Maurice watched as Miranda and Stacy caused another stir outside the restaurant before being driven away.

"Nothing to report out here," Maurice said. "So, how are we going to get that USB from the safe?"

"We?" Dom tilted his head. "You mean how am *I* going to risk my job to get that USB?"

"Boys, boys," Nille butted in. "I've got it all planned out. Dom, how about a lunch date tomorrow?"

CHAPTER
EIGHTEEN

When they were young, Dom, Maurice, and Kendra had a ritual whenever they played video games against each other. After a round, the winner would hide the loser's controller somewhere in the house. Whoever found the controller would be the next to challenge the winner. Dom recalled what it felt like to scramble around the house looking in every potential hiding spot, desperate to be the one plopped in front of the TV with a controller in his hands. He felt similarly sitting at work knowing that hanging somewhere over his head was the USB stick in Stacy's third floor office.

At lunch time, Dom hurried over to the café where Nille said to meet her. A tinge of disappointment hit him as he saw Francis sitting at a table in the back corner instead, nose buried in a book.

"Nille sends her apologies," he said, placing his book down as Dom sat across from him. "Axel had an urgent need for her tech skills, but I was given instructions to run down with you."

"Great." Dom wrung his hands.

"Nervous?" Francis asked with a hint of amusement.

"Well, I've never done a heist before, so, yeah," Dom answered. A part of him wanted to back out, but he was too curious at this point. The Village had been right about Webb's trip to the city and had successfully coordinated the USB handoff, so it was only right to know what was on it.

"I would correct your use of the term 'heist,' but I know you take issue with how we describe our actions." Francis reached down and produced a small black drawstring bag that he slid across the table. "Everything you'll need is in there."

Dom looked around at the sparsely occupied café before opening the bag. He saw black gloves, a tweezer-like instrument, a tiny black box, and a rectangular piece of plastic about the size of the beeper his dad used to carry.

"The larger box is the key to your task, literally. It's a device that will unlock the safe," Francis explained. "Don't ask me how. If you have any questions, Nille will be in your ear. You'll find an earbud in the smaller box. She'll take you through the whole process. You know, make sure you don't set off any alarms or anything. You also have tools to pick door locks, and the gloves are self-explanatory."

Dom tightened the bag back closed. "So, when am I supposed to be doing all this?" he asked.

"You'll be working overtime tonight," Francis said. "Nille said to stay in the building after hours to get this done."

THE AFTERNOON CREPT ALONG SLOWLY. Maintaining focus in his sessions was a challenge as Dom kept thinking about how he would pull off this mission. While his clients explored their Haven modules, he imagined all the ways things could go wrong.

Amalia came by his office near the end of the day, asking when he was heading home. "I have a bunch of notes to finish, so I'm gonna stick around for a little to knock them out," he told her.

As five o'clock hit, anxiety seeped into his pores, settling in his gut. After a half hour of fidgeting and looking at his unchanging laptop screen, a call buzzed his leg. He inserted the earbud.

"Hiiii! Ready to go stealth mode?"

"Your enthusiasm for theft isn't unexpected for a hacker, but still a little troubling, Nille."

"A little bit of trouble never hurt anyone."

"Since I'm the one at risk here, I'll be the judge of that." This wasn't the typical mischief like what he would get into when he was younger. He'd never even thought of doing anything that could lead to prison time.

"Don't worry, I'm going to make this as easy as possible for you," Nille said. She gave a quick rundown of the plan. "For now, you just hang out in your office for a bit. Let the building clear out. It'll also give me time to shut down the security cameras."

Not sure what else to do, he closed his office door, turned out the light, and crouched under his desk. This was typically when he would yell at the character in a movie that they were making a stupid decision, but now that he was the one put in a tricky situation all he could do was wait.

"Anyone else on the line?" he asked.

There was a stretch of silence before Nille answered. "Charles is on another line; he's keeping watch nearby for anyone who may enter the building. Just us on this one though." Another pause before she muttered to herself, "Okay, first step done."

"Sorry, didn't mean to interrupt the security hack."

"All good. I've been getting into these types of systems since middle school. So, what's up?"

Dom adjusted his position under the desk, already feeling a knot forming near his right shoulder blade. "How do you know you're doing the right thing?"

"Well, corporate security systems haven't really changed much in basic format over the years so it's pretty easy—"

"No, no, not that. Well, kinda. I mean, as part of The Village, when you're doing things like this that can land you in trouble, how do you decide to do it anyway? Do you feel free even knowing there's so much at stake?"

"Free? Did I miss something?"

"It was what Maurice told me last night. That he felt more free being away from the things weighing him down and by contributing to your cause. Do you feel free?"

"Mmm, gotcha. Each of us learns something from our maroon lineage as members of The Village. Your cousin connected to the idea of fleeing as the path of freedom. I'm personally drawn to what it takes to establish freedom. The maroons created a space for possibility in a time when it was unimaginable. I feel like I'm doing the same every time I code or I figure out a new exploit. I do this to make things possible for people who have never seen otherwise."

What was his purpose in doing this? He couldn't settle with the idea that all his training to become a therapist had culminated in this moment of being hunched under his desk, ready to steal from his first employer. But if Atlasal was planning to do anything to make life in Parkside harder, he had to know.

"Alright, cameras are down," Nille said. "By Charles' count all employees have left the building. It's go-time."

Dom took a deep breath before leaving from underneath his desk. When he opened his door, he was greeted with a blanket of darkness. "Yeah, looks empty to me."

"The only lights that should be on now are the ones in the stairwell," Nille said. "Make your way over there and up to Stacy's office. This is the quick and easy part."

The light from his phone provided a guide as Dom made his way across the abandoned first floor. Passing through the conference room, he thought about Louis' comment to Stacy about his work ethic, wondering how Louis would characterize his current actions to her. A square of light came into view, leading him to the stairwell.

At the landing for the second floor, he looked to his right, instinctively checking for Amalia, whose office could be seen easily from the stairwell. Suddenly, the top of a broom stick wobbled into sight. Dom jerked back out of sight of the hunched, gray-haired janitor, bumping his shoulder against the wall.

"Hello?" the janitor called out.

Dom darted down the stairs as quickly and gently as he could. At the bottom, he cut left and went under a table in the conference room. "What the hell? I thought the building was empty! One of the cleaning staff almost spotted me." He tapped the earbud repeatedly.

"Damn it, I'm sorry, Dom," Nille sounded annoyed. "Charles said he saw the usual two-person cleaning crew leave, but they must have had an extra person with them today. I'm having him handle it now."

A loud banging started from the direction of the front entrance. The janitor skidded out the stairwell, broom in hand. "Hey! What is that? Who's there? I'll call the police!" He took out his phone as he cautiously stepped toward the lobby.

"The fucking cops?" Dom sputtered. "I can't do this."

"You can and you will," Nille directed. "Remember everyone who's counting on you."

Dom bit the inside of his lip. Ignoring what his brain was telling him, he seized the window of opportunity, hurrying back to the stairwell. He bounded up two steps at a time to the third floor. Quickly, he reached for the lockpick. To his surprise, as he placed his hand on the handle to Stacy's office, ready to take Nille's instruction, it turned and the door opened with a slight creak.

"What the hell? Why is her office unlocked? This has to be a trap," Dom said hesitantly.

"You're the psychological expert, right?" Nille said. "Stacy's been out of town for weeks. Maybe she's not back in her usual routine yet and simply forgot to lock her door."

"Nah, something's not right."

"Look, you're in, so take advantage of the moment. Do you see the safe?" Nille's tone was hardened with focus.

There was a cabinet beneath the drawers of Stacy's desk. Opening it, Dom laid eyes on the black safe. "Yeah, got it."

"Okay. Now, just place the rectangular device you were given over the number pad. It's going to provide you with the passcode by reading heat signatures to tell the order the numbers were pressed in."

He placed the device over the number pad, holding it in place. It beeped several times before displaying the four-digit passcode. Dom typed the numbers in, the sound of a pressure release signaling the loosening of the lock mechanism. He opened the safe; the USB stick lay there by itself. "Okay, what do I do again?"

"Pull that tab on the bottom of the device."

Dom examined the device, finding what Nille had described. He flicked the tab with his thumb nail, opening a slot. "Got it, downloading the data now."

He inserted the USB into the hidden slot, and waited the few minutes it took for the data transfer to complete. "Alright, I'm outta here." He placed the USB back in the safe just as he'd found it, closed the office door, and ran out of the building.

Out front, his hurried pace caused him to slip on something, barely catching himself before he landed on his side. Looking back, he saw the top foot of a broomstick, jagged at the end. "How exactly did Charles handle that problem with the janitor?"

"I don't know. Not important," Nille said bluntly. "Hurry up and bring the data over."

CHAPTER

NINETEEN

DOM COULDN'T SHAKE FEELING LIKE HE WAS BEING watched following the heist. New Horizons told staff the next day to take extra precaution because one of the cleaning crew was assaulted outside the building after hours. Stacy was briefly in the office a couple days later and all he felt like doing was hiding under his desk again.

The weekend offered little reprieve from his paranoia, as word came through that The Village had finally accessed the info on the USB. It took Nille days to break through what turned out to be a surprisingly well protected file storage system. As much as Dom wanted to know what they'd found out, he couldn't help but think that this knowledge would act as a glaring target on his back. Part of him hoped there was nothing to worry about, that Atlasal wasn't doing anything nefarious.

The energy that met him inside the Village hideout contradicted his hope. Something serious was going on. For the first time since he'd been introduced to The Village, the whole crew was assembled. Maurice greeted him first.

"Cuz, hurry up," he said as he put an arm around Dom's shoulder. It wasn't a comforting gesture, more like a bulldozer trying to push a mound of dirt to a desired location.

In the corner of the room, Dom saw Charles sitting on a crate, arms crossed and head down, appearing to be asleep. "Hey!" He shook Maurice off him. Charles glanced up. "What did you do to that janitor? I didn't know beating people up was part of the gig. I'd rather get caught sneaking around than get someone hurt."

Charles stood. "Sometimes you have to make tough decisions."

"That's it? No remorse?"

Francis zipped past, flipping through a book on urban planning. "We don't have time to get into analyses of violence, and you don't have the time to worry about what anybody else has done or will do again when necessary. Bigger things are happening." He continued into a back room.

Dom threw his arms up in frustration.

"Look, he's right," Maurice said. "We need to get you up to speed so you can understand what's going on." He took Dom back to a dark office where Nille and Axel were looking at a map of Selton City projected onto a wall.

"That's the only way this could work. It's sick," Axel said to Nille as the cousins entered.

Nille looked up from her computer. "Hey, guys, we're just digging deeper into the situation we have on our hands. Dom, you should take a seat so I can break everything down to you."

Suddenly, Dom was only able to take in short breaths. This was it, what he'd been waiting for. His head felt cloudy as he sat down. Nille dragged windows across the projected screen while anticipation jittered through his body. He looked over at Maurice, whose eyes had become a void.

"Atlasal really upped the security measures for these files. Now that I know what was in them, it makes sense," Nille said. "Hate to admit it, but I had to hit up a connect to help me crack through everything. We've been scrambling ever since I uncovered what Webb and her people have been keeping under wraps."

"What is it?" Dom ventured to ask.

Axel stepped forward, coming alongside the projected image. "It has to do with the Haven program." A chart came up on the wall, depicting sales projections for Atlasal's headset along with a proposal for selling the Haven program separately for other hardware systems to further boost revenue. "At the surface level, Atlasal's partnership with New Horizons was just a pilot project for Haven. What we didn't know was the end goal of the project. What we found brings everything together, including the data from Atlasal's drone and e-scooter. They were surveying the land."

A document was pulled up, the title page reading, A2: Our New Horizon. "What's A2?" Dom asked. Nille scrolled down to the executive summary of the document.

"It's the code name for Atlasal's second headquarters," Axel explained.

"I didn't know they have two. Where is it?" Dom tried to sound genuine in his question, but knew he was only asking to prolong the clear truth.

"It doesn't exist yet," Axel answered. "But it will. Here in Selton City."

"In Parkside to be exact," Maurice added, rubbing his temples. "It's all a set up!"

"Yes. The competition New Horizons is running with you and your co-workers is just a way to quickly prove Haven's viability and thus profitability." Axel motioned for Nille to bring back the chart. "By demonstrating how quickly users show improvement, Atlasal will be able to progress on to greater investment and wider distribution, using the profits to fund the building of their new headquarters."

"Where are they going to build in Parkside? They haven't even been able to add another grocery store for years." Again, Dom asked only to try to give room for some explanation other than the obvious.

Axel continued. "The city is making it easier for them to seize land; we've seen the communications with the mayor. It's early in the process, but the first land purchase could be announced by the end of the year. Construction won't start for a while, but just the prospect of Atlasal coming to the area is going to raise property taxes and price everyone out of the neighborhood. It will be a slow pushout, but a devastating one." Nille put the city map back on the wall side-by-side with an overhead view of the proposed area where Atlasal planned to build A2. The plot of land ran right up against Randolph Road.

It was like the floor fell from underneath him. Detached from his surroundings, Dom stared blankly at the map of the only place he had ever called home. Thinking about his family, friends, and community being forced to leave stunned him. His parents had put so much work into their house. The people in the community did so much to support each other, but what could they do against this looming threat?

Maurice placed a hand on his shoulder. "I know it's a lot to take in. We're going to stop them, though. We have to."

Dom didn't budge. It was slowly dawning on him the role he had played in the catastrophe being brought upon Parkside. Every time he initiated the Haven program, planting his clients into virtual worlds, he'd unwittingly been gradually whisking them away from their actual homes. "I have to stop them. I have to stop everyone from using Haven."

Axel exhaled, shaking her head. "Even if you could, it's too late."

Dom straightened against the chair.

"There's only a month left until Webb returns to Selton City to finalize preliminary plans for A2 with Stacy and the mayor," Axel said.

"And, based on info we got from a little bug," Nille added, "the results Stacy received at the first contest check-in already exceed the necessary trajectory to meet their goal to expand distribution."

Louis came to Dom's mind. He bet that his co-worker's found zeal for Haven was the push past the threshold. And he would probably win the contest as predicted, meeting Miranda Webb as she plotted to reshape the city. The whole scheme was manipulation at the highest degree. "So, what, we just clear everyone out of Parkside to make way for Atlasal's summer home?"

"We're working as fast as we can to come up with solutions." Francis leaned against the wall, book under his arm. "I've been looking into possible legal challenges to the project. Problem is, displacement has been a protected practice since this land was claimed through the violence of invaders centuries ago."

"Why would the mayor agree to this?" Dom asked. "Selling out the people she's supposed to represent."

"*Selling* is the keyword," Francis responded. "When big companies come into a community, they often promise things like giving money to local organizations, creating job training programs, and having their employees volunteer in the community to make their presence seem positive while covering up the harmful ramifications. No politician would pass on that level of an illusion."

"So, it's us against the billion-dollar company," Dom said, resignation coloring his voice.

"There's always an opportunity to resist." Charles lurched around the corner, joining the group. "We just gotta figure out the best way to fight back."

"I don't want you to do any more fighting," Dom raised his voice as he stood up.

Maurice stepped in front of him. "Chill out, man. If Charles wasn't there the other night, we wouldn't even have this information to argue about." Arms folded, a glint of gold flashed from Charles' mouth as he let out a confirmatory huff.

Dom's chest pressed against his cousin's shoulder as he tried to push forward. "Don't try to excuse what he did. The janitor didn't deserve that."

"We need to focus on what the people of Parkside deserve, which is to remain right where they are." Axel took command of the room again. Dom stepped back from Maurice, turning to listen to her. "As daunting as this task seems right now, the challenge lies at the heart of The Village's ethos. Our maroon predecessors knew what it meant to exist in the in between. To be in and out of place simultaneously. There was purpose in this delicate existence. But, Parkside residents have not planned their relocation, it is being decided for them. Whatever we do next, our attention has to stay on the people, not on disputes between each other. Every moment wasted on bickering is time Atlasal is using to move their plans forward. We can't allow that."

Still left with the dilemma of continuing to use Haven, Dom contemplated his options. If he stopped going to work, he'd be fired. If he went to work and refused to use Haven, he'd be fired. Raising some type of concern to Amalia crossed his mind until her position in all this became clear. The snippets of conversations he'd overheard the past couple months now seemed to point toward her being used as a tool to push the implementation of Haven to ensure its success. There was likely no way for her to push back against Atlasal, either. He struggled to figure out his next move.

Suddenly, his phone dinged with a notification that inadvertently made a decision for him. He'd set an alert for the name, hoping blogs or social media were keeping up with the story more than the local news.

JASMINE HENRY: FOUND AND RETURNED HOME.

CHAPTER
TWENTY

Dom managed to wait until exactly nine a.m. on Monday to call Ms. Henry. No answer. Four more calls throughout the day and still nothing. The news that night finally made a brief mention of Jasmine being found, breezing past the story like it was a simple traffic update.

The next day, he was in supervision with Amalia when a text from Ms. Henry finally came through. She was in the lobby with Jasmine. He shot up out of his chair.

"Hold on!" Amalia motioned for Dom to sit. "Let's plan this out first. What's your approach going to be with Jasmine?"

For all the anguish her absence had put him through, he hadn't thought about what he would say once she returned. He had been dreading the thought that she wouldn't be found. "I need to know what happened. Where she went, what she did, who she was with."

"You're not the police," Amalia stated. "Let them do their job and you focus on yours. You're not wrong to want the context of what happened, but your role is to help her process the impact of this time on her and her mother. How do you plan to incorporate Haven into this?"

At the mention of the program, Dom tightened up. He wasn't sure if he was successful in softening the glare aimed at Amalia. Her ability to push Atlasal's product regardless of the situation was absurd. He wondered if she knew about A2. "I was thinking of not using the headset today. We haven't met for a month; we need the face-to-face time."

"Why would you do that?" Amalia shot back. "There's so much that can be incorporated into the virtual exercises now. Haven doesn't even need the whole breakdown of events; just input that the client has been missing for a month and it will come up with something you could never think of. You're behind enough in the standings to want to get as much data in your hands as possible."

Data. Like all there was to Jasmine was a collection of symptoms, information to be parsed and applied in ways best fit for the profits of a tech conglomerate. She was nothing more than the slop feeding the growth of a grotesque creature.

"Atlasal can wait. They've gotten enough out of us already."

"This is something everybody signed up for, Dom," she said despite the truth that he had no clue about the Atlasal partnership before getting the job at New Horizons. "I know this case has gotten under your skin, but there's no need to be so resistant. Just follow the protocol."

"Gotten under my skin?" Dom leaned forward as words began to escape his mouth. "Jasmine went missing twice! How was I supposed to react? I kept it together as best I could over this past month, but I can't just be a pawn like you."

Amalia's eye twitched. She stayed silent for a moment, typing on her computer. "You know," she started, pulling a piece of lint from her blouse, "there's so much I could say right now to explain everything I've been through in my career. To unnecessarily and redundantly justify my choices. Instead of continuing to waste my breath, I'm going to schedule a meeting with Stacy for when she's in the office next. You can explain your disagreements to her." Dom left the room without another word.

In the lobby, Dom encountered a very different scene from when Jasmine first went missing. No one was yelling, and Jasmine wasn't being held close by her hood. Instead, she and her mom sat with a couple of chairs between them. Ms. Henry appeared distant in another way; withdrawn, almost sinking into herself as she stared off at nothing. Jasmine on the other hand seemed oddly normal. Nothing in her demeanor indicated she had been through any stressful experience. Only the frayed condition of her braids revealed she had been on her own for a while. By looking at her, he couldn't tell how she felt about being back home.

"Hey there," he said, standing between the two.

Jasmine looked up then glanced over at her mom quickly as if to check if she could respond first. "Hi, Mr. Dom. Sorry I missed our last few sessions." She stared at her shoes.

"I'm glad you're back," Dom said to Jasmine. "And that you're safe. Let's all head back to my office so we can get caught up."

Dom tried to engage Ms. Henry once they were at his office. "Can we speak first? I know you've been through a lot, so I want to make sure you have a chance to process everything."

"My daughter has been gone for a whole month!" Ms. Henry's eyes bored deep into his own. "She won't tell the police anything and she wants me to act like everything's all good. You're the therapist, so you talk to her and figure out what's going on!" She dropped into a chair outside his office, disappearing into her phone.

Dom gave an awkward nod to her before proceeding into his office with Jasmine.

Jasmine quickly snatched the VR headset from Dom's desk, loosening the straps to place it over her head.

"Nope, not today," Dom said, taking the headset from her. "No hiding behind these goggles." He placed it behind a plant on the bookshelf.

"Fine," she huffed. "I'll tell you what you want to know. I was in Selton the whole time, no one touched me, no one hurt me, no one sold me. One of my friends—former friend now—snitched and that's how the police found me. Can I do the VR now?"

"We're not using that anymore!" Dom cleared his throat and continued, calmer. "VR isn't going to help right now, so let's move on. I'm happy that you're in one piece, but you're not just going to skate through the story like that. It's not my job to investigate, but I do need to know some things if I'm going to be helpful at all. Why did you leave this time?" He sighed when all she did was shrug in response.

She took heed of his impatience and spoke. "I didn't make some big plan to disappear or even stay gone for that long. Once I was with my friends, I just didn't want to go back. Instead of being cooped up with Mom, I could be free and have fun."

The similarity of her words to Maurice's own explanation of how it felt to be away from Parkside bothered him. A middle schooler's desire for freedom didn't measure up to what Maurice had been through and it was still hard for Dom to accept his cousin's rationale. The impact on the people left behind, like him, was too much.

"Fun. I don't have to tell you that your mom hasn't had any fun in the last month. It wasn't fun for me to go looking for you all over the city when I heard the news, either." He heard himself sounding more like a parent than a therapist.

"No one asked you to do all that," Jasmine shot back.

"I couldn't just sit back and let that happen again." He knew he was referencing Maurice just as much as Jasmine's repeat runaway. "I might just be your therapist, but your safety is important to me."

"If you're just gonna go on and on like this, then I don't' think I need to be here." She got up, heading for the door. Something fell from her back pocket.

"What's this?" Dom asked, picking up what looked like a business card. One side had hearts hand-drawn in black ink sprinkled across a white background. On the opposite, a strange symbol was printed. Against another white background was a thickly outlined five-pointed star. Right under the tip of each point was an eye. The eye up top was open, while the other four were closed.

Jasmine rushed over, reaching for the card. "It's not yours. Give it back!" He held it away from her. "Stop! Give it back!"

Clearly the card meant something to her. "Tell me what it is and I'll give it back," Dom said, again sounding parental.

"A kid gave it to *me*, so it's none of your business," Jasmine said, arms crossed as she rocked from foot to foot.

What kid has business cards? A fear ran through Dom that someone had tried to recruit Jasmine for purposes she was unaware of. "How old was this kid? What did they say this star meant? Did they give anyone else a card?"

Jasmine shook her head. "I already told you nobody touched or tried to sell me. I'm not being trafficked. The kid's name was Brady or Brody, I don't know, some kind of white boy name. I met him a couple weeks ago at a par...at a friend's house. He said he was new to the area and would be going to my school this year. We don't have a lot of white kids at school, but he seemed pretty cool." She looked down, biting the inside of her cheek to hold off a smile.

Dom turned the card back over to the hearts. "Cool, uh-huh. So, what about the card?"

Jasmine shrugged. "He said his older brother is a graphic designer. It's just a logo they made together, playing around. He gave it to me so I'd remember who he is when school starts."

While everything she said sounded plausible, there seemed to be much more to the situation.

"Can I go now?"

He relented, handing the card back allowing Jasmine to leave. The grilling he took from Ms. Henry for the short session was so harsh, he couldn't get a word in about his concerns and worried about them coming back.

Upset that the session hadn't gone as expected, Dom grabbed the VR headset from the bookshelf. He wanted to test Amalia's suggestion. He brought up the tutorial mode on his tablet, typed "client missing for one month," and waited for Haven to run its analysis. The virtual scenario was fully generated once Dom had the headset on. He turned in a full circle, looking at the empty interior of a house. His digitized voice read out instructions to him, stating that there was an inventory of items he could scroll through. The task was to populate the house with whatever items would make him feel the safest.

Dom browsed through the categories of standard furniture and appliances, a surprisingly broad selection of food to stock the house with, and various specialty items like games and pets. The activity was simple, but he understood the intention of it. Allow Jasmine to create her own version of safety in order to identify what she may need to prevent future instances of running away. Still, he couldn't help seeing the empty house and thinking of the thousands of people who would be moved out of their homes once Atlasal began implementing their plan.

CHAPTER
TWENTY-ONE

On Friday, Amalia followed through on her promise. Dom dragged his feet like cinderblocks as he plodded up to the third floor. This time he had permission, a requirement, to be in Stacy's office, but he was in no rush.

He entered, looking around as if it were his first time in there. It did seem more spacious without the constraining pressure of stealing secret information. Amalia and Stacy sat close to each other sharing a laugh, one lively enough that Stacy put her hand on Amalia's knee to steady herself. When she attended the first contest leaderboard event, it was as if Stacy didn't know and didn't want to know Amalia. What had turned them so friendly?

"Have a seat." A knot formed in Dom's stomach as Stacy quickly shifted from amusement to demanding. "Thank you, Amalia, for setting up this meeting today. Please, start us off if you have anything to say to your supervisee, but I would like some time to speak to him alone." She glared deep into his eyes as if daring him to speak.

"I think I've done all I've been asked to do up to this point." Amalia stood, came around the side of Stacy's desk, and sat back against it in front of Dom. She spoke to him with a sense of smugness. "As I mentioned in our last supervision meeting, I don't feel the need to justify anything on my end. If there is anything you need to explain, I'll allow Ms. Connors to be the one to hear you out." She turned and gave Stacy a quick downward nod with a slight smile before leaving her office.

"I'm glad we made time for this sit down," Stacy said, turning her phone face down on the desk. "Where should we begin? Tell me why you're here today."

Dom swallowed, trying to combat his suddenly dry throat. "Um, yes. Amalia set up this meeting after I told her I didn't want to use Haven in a session with one of my clients."

Stacy flitted her hand by her head, sweeping away his words. "Yes, of course. I'm aware of that. What I mean is why are you *here* today if you have such a big issue with how this organization runs?" She remained laser-focused on Dom, waiting for an answer.

"My decision to not use Haven with my client didn't have anything to do with New Horizons or Atlasal, it was all about what was best for her in that moment. After being missing for a month, it didn't seem reasonable to have her do a virtual reality exercise right away."

Stacy turned to her computer monitor, clicking the mouse once. "I'm wondering if you came to that conclusion so easily because you've had the worst Haven scores out of all your colleagues. Looking at your numbers, you started off strong. Amalia said you were pretty fully committed to the program at first. But you had a significant fall off about a month and a half ago. Do you think your clients have not been improving due to a flaw with Haven?"

The image of paper slips with red lettering falling from trees filled Dom's mind as he thought back to the moment that sent his suspicions about Atlasal over the edge. "No, I mean, I don't really know how to answer that. I have a good rapport with all my clients. Their outcome scores may not be changing in the way the company wants to see, but I know I'm not providing bad therapy."

"So, then according to that equation it's still a problem with Haven." She sighed, clasping her hands together over her knee. "You know, Miranda and I had long talks about this partnership and how it would succeed. As women, we've both battled our way through the fields of tech and healthcare, having our ideas challenged at every possible chance along the way. She could tell you herself how the billionaire title only led to more scrutiny. So, understand that when she decided to expand Atlasal into healthcare and chose me—chose us and this community—to be their first partner, we knew it would be difficult. But, the power of this product kept us pushing forward. We need everyone working on our teams to give that same push. If you think you can provide better care without us, tell me why you should remain a part of this team."

Although Dom knew what was really driving the business partnership, the determination he heard from Stacy was still striking. It was clear she believed wholeheartedly in what she was doing. He tried to mount a defense. "I hear you. I understand my performance hasn't been the best representation of what you—what we are working to accomplish here. If you give me a chance, I can fix my mistakes."

"What about Reggie? Was that a mistake?" Her face steeled.

Dom racked his brain. "Who? I'm not sure what you're talking about?"

"People assume CEOs are detached from their companies. My time away from the office may make it seem like I don't care, but all of our staff are important. That includes our janitor of ten years, Reggie."

Shocked at the accusation, Dom threw his arms out. "What? You think I beat up our janitor?" Internally, he cursed Charles for what he did and for being so nonchalant about it. He was furious that it was now all falling on him.

"I'm not saying you did. I just know you were the only employee here late enough that day to have crossed paths with him." She turned her computer monitor to Dom.

He felt bricks in his stomach as he looked at a date and time-stamped black and white image of himself, mid-pace as he ascended past the second-floor landing in the stairwell. He thought Nille had cut all the security cameras.

"Our security system didn't show anything, but I've felt the need for more safeguarding recently and had some independent cameras installed." A streak of enjoyment flashed across her face. "What were you doing that night? Why did you need to come up here after hours? It's only my office on this floor."

It was like he'd been asked to solve a riddle. "That doesn't...I think there's...if I could..."

She put a hand up. "Your answer doesn't matter. Far less is required to terminate employees. For you, refusal to follow company treatment practices along with snooping around the office after dark makes the decision a no-brainer. You're to have your things out of the building within the next hour." She turned her phone to look at the screen, then looked back at him. "You know, I had no expectation our conversation today would change my mind, but I did secretly hope to at least feel like we were losing a good person. Guess I'll add this to your list of underwhelming outcomes."

Dom was speechless, but not because he didn't have anything to say. He wanted to curse out Stacy and tell her how much of a bad person *she* was for plotting to destroy his community. He was left in despair as he departed from Stacy's presence, wondering just how he could stop New Horizons and Atlasal's plan without being on the inside anymore.

On the second floor, he stopped to look around for any sign of the camera that had caught him. Nothing stood out. With her direct view of the stairwell, Amalia came up to him before he continued downstairs. In a tone more reminiscent of the first time they met than what she'd displayed in Stacy's office, Amalia said softly, "I'm sorry things had to end like this."

"Are you? You seem to have gotten closer with the boss. Has she told you what Haven is really all about yet?"

She exhaled, letting his question dissipate between them. "Goodbye, Dom."

The door to the lobby swung back just as Dom was about to open it. Louis appeared. "Another successful session. Only a few weeks left in this thing; no one's gonna catch me." He put his fist out for a pound, but had to complete the action himself when Dom didn't return the favor.

"I just got fired." The statement didn't feel real yet.

"What? No way!" Despite his obsession with winning the contest, there seemed to be genuine concern in his voice.

"Yeah, by Stacy herself."

"What happened?"

Dom didn't even know where to begin in answering that. "Look, I don't have time to get into everything right now. Just...just be careful here, Louis. I know you feel like you're doing great things. And you are!" He paused. "What I mean is, I'm sure your clients are benefitting from working with you, but there's more to this Atlasal thing. I think you were right to be skeptical in the beginning."

Louis looked confused. "Bro, I'm sorry things went so downhill for you. I appreciate you trying to look out for me, but I see a lot of opportunity here. Maybe once you've had some time to process everything, you'll see things differently." He patted Dom on the shoulder as he left him alone.

As Dom stepped outside with his belongings and looked up pensively at the New Horizons sign, his phone sounded with another alert. He dropped his phone as soon as he read the news on the screen.

He stood frozen in place. People passed him on the sidewalk with puzzled looks. A woman's mouth moved, perhaps asking if he was okay, but the sound didn't reach him. If it had, his answer would be obvious.

No.

He was not okay and wasn't sure if he ever would be again. The alert whirled through his mind, warping his senses.

JASMINE HENRY FOUND DEAD.

CHAPTER
TWENTY-TWO

No matter how many times he read the details, the reality would not sink in.

Found in an alley behind a dumpster.

Marks on her neck suggesting strangling.

He just saw her a few days ago. Had she run away again? He was overwhelmed, but he needed answers. Even if he found out what happened, nothing would change. She was gone. He knew it was self-centered to blame himself. He was not the culprit, nor her savior. Still, the possibility of somehow changing her path clung to him as he found himself at The Village hideout hours later.

It seemed like the only place to go. The only place he could talk about everything that transpired. The words refused to form in his throat, though. All he could do was hold his phone up to Maurice, showing him the news.

"Holy shit." Maurice scratched his head. "Do you have any idea who could've done this?"

It took a moment for the question to register. His whole world had flipped upside down in less than twenty-four hours. "I don't know…In our last session I had concerns about this kid she met, but I…I don't know." His mind was clouded.

"It's possible that law enforcement is going to ask for her treatment records to learn more about what was going on in her life," Maurice speculated. "You think Atlasal will let them access Haven?"

Dom wanted answers, too, but Maurice's dive into crime solving agitated him. He didn't realize what happened to Jasmine is exactly the kind of thing Dom and his parents thought could have happened to him. The emotional toll of the situation at hand didn't seem to faze Maurice. Dom struggled to look him in the eyes as he explained what else happened that day. "I don't have an answer to that question and I have no way of finding out now. I got fired today." Maurice stared at him, dumbfounded.

Dom recounted the conversation with Stacy.

"Damn, an extra camera? Nille is thorough, but there's always a chance for unknown factors with a mission like that."

"I'm not blaming her," Dom said. "I feel like Stacy set me up. Like she knew I was going to steal the USB that night."

"You said she fired you for snooping around, though. Did she accuse you of actually stealing anything? Did she even know you were in her office?"

Dom paused. "No, she didn't say anything about stealing, but I doubt she only had a camera in the stairwell. She has to know I got to her safe."

"But then why fire you if she knows you have the information about Atlasal's plans? Wouldn't it be better to keep you close and make sure you keep quiet?"

The possibilities swam through Dom's head. "I hear you, I just...nothing is making a lot of sense right now. I can't get into Stacy's mind. I can't get into New Horizons. Jasmine's dead and there's nothing I can do about it."

Dom pictured himself standing on the other side of a moat from his now former place of work, forbidden entry. The lost advantage of his inside position aside, he'd essentially failed at his first job post-grad school. Maybe Francis was right. What good was he doing there, anyway? Nothing he'd done kept Jasmine from her fate.

A sudden realization swelled inside of him. Sure, he needed to be at New Horizons to uncover Atlasal's plans, but the walls of that office were more confining than he had initially understood. He thought about Maurice's appeal to collective action as a response to individual circumstances. Now that he was out from under the watch of Stacy, New Horizons, and Atlasal, he had room to maneuver and try a different approach.

"I want to join The Village. Officially."

A look crossed Maurice's face that Dom hadn't seen in a long time. Growing up, Maurice wasn't quite the type to let his athletic ability define who he was, but he was confident. Whenever Dom made a comment about being faster than him or teased that he could snatch an interception from him, Maurice would raise his chin up and lower his eyelids as he looked down at Dom in quiet disagreement. It was this faint squint that Dom picked up on briefly now, as if the idea of him joining The Village was offensive in some way.

Before any response came from Maurice, Axel entered the room.

"And what made you decide that?" she asked.

Dom looked back and forth, unsure how much she had overheard. "Well, you guys brought me here as a recruit, right? Now I'm saying I want to be a part of this for real."

Axel replied, "You've been pretty reluctant to carry out tasks for us, seemingly only sticking around to be with your cousin. What has brought this change of mind about?"

Dom told her about Jasmine and getting fired.

She buried her face in her hands, muttering to herself. "Oh dear. So so young. I'm sorry, Dom." She dropped into a squat, balancing on the balls of her feet, weighed down by the news. "And losing New Horizons...things are getting serious."

"Yes, and you need to be serious about this," Maurice said to Dom. "I initially suggested bringing you in because of your proximity to Atlasal. I haven't been convinced though that you can live out our ethos. Joining The Village is not a light decision to make on a whim. Are you prepared to disconnect from the people around you? You might want to have more time with me, but is the tradeoff worth it?"

His words stung. Dom disagreed that he would have to abandon everyone in his life like Maurice had. There was another way to go about this. "This is about our home, Maurice. I've been wrong about a lot, okay. Wrong about you in some ways. Despite my disagreements with certain tactics, my time with you all has shown me the possibilities beyond what I know. With our community in danger, I'm admitting that joining The Village is the best way forward."

Maurice stood briskly. "Look, Axel ultimately calls the shots on new members. If she wants to let you in, she'll give you the initiation details. If you make it through the process, I guess I'll have nothing to argue about." He gave one more doubtful look at Dom before walking away.

CHAPTER
TWENTY-THREE

Keep. Give. Burn.

Axel's instructions were simple. He was to bring three items to The Village initiation ceremony. The item to keep had to be something that symbolized transformation, what he would become as a member of The Village. Another would be gifted to The Village as a sign of gratitude. The final item represented something he needed to let go of in order to commit to the values of the group.

Surprisingly, the item to burn was the easiest to choose. Staring at it on his apartment's bedroom wall, his ornately framed graduate school diploma maintained the façade of a prized possession. It was odd how only a few months removed from graduation his outlook had changed so drastically. A sense of embarrassment came on as he thought about how tightly he had clung to his Master's level studies only to see the field he saw as the path toward helping his community be used to rip it apart.

His item to gift stood in direct contrast to his diploma. At his core, Dom truly wanted to be a helper, a healer, but it had become something he imposed on those around him. He had become so sure of his abilities, driven by a need to feel effective, that his approach was more self-focused, meant to prove how good he was at what he did. As part of The Village, he would need to be different, to be more connected to those he was helping. His parents' house held the item representing this connection.

Their eyes were full of sympathy when he walked in.

"We caught the news yesterday. Heard about a young girl who was murdered. She'd run away from home recently. That's not..." his mom trailed off, waiting for him to confirm their suspicion.

"Yeah, it's her."

"My God. I'm so sorry, Dom." His dad embraced him.

"I'm guessing that's why you asked if you could have this," his mom said, picking up Maurice's Senior Day picture from the table behind her. She cradled the frame like it was a royal heirloom. Like she didn't want her fingertips to touch her nephew's despondent face.

"No, I just need some things for my apartment. To make it feel more comfortable." He didn't want to let them know he'd been fired and didn't want to talk about Jasmine anymore, so he escaped to the office upstairs, Maurice's picture in hand.

"Does the copier still work?" Dom called down, fidgeting with the machine's cord, plugging it into the outlet closest to the desk. The power button didn't light up when pushed.

"Oh, I don't know. It's been in a box longer than it's been out. You know we don't use that room much," his mom said.

Dom quickly stopped in his room to grab the other initiation item. When he came back downstairs, his mom shifted as she tried to avoid looking at Maurice's picture.

"It's strange, you know. At times, the thing I miss the most is taking care of him," she said. She hadn't said anything this direct about Maurice in years. "He was affected so deeply when Grace died. I mean, we all were. But caring for him gave me hope that he would be able to grow through the experience and become the type of person he maybe couldn't see for himself at the time." She wiped at the corner of her eye. "Go ahead and take the original. We can make a copy another time."

***

By the following night, Dom still didn't quite feel mentally prepared for the initiation. Certainly, it felt better to be sitting before the five Villagers without being tied up, but the atmosphere was similar to that first night. There was a sense that although it was his initiation ceremony, he was not welcome there. They all stood like black-clad statues around a large metal bowl and raised pedestal. Dom imagined his diploma aflame, creating a bonfire in the bowl. The image unexpectedly eased his nerves.

Axel spoke, "For centuries, The Village has added to its ranks for the purpose of expanding its capacity to deliver healing liberation wherever it has taken root. Tonight, we continue that legacy with you, Freedom Hall."

"We will begin the ceremony with the presentation of the Three Treasures," Axel explained. "Please, share with us your Treasure Found."

Luckily, his mom was not one to do away with the trinkets of his childhood. In the toy chest still tucked away in his bedroom closet he'd found a scattering of lettered wooden blocks, only about a quarter of the alphabet remaining. He'd taken the one with the letter K. "This is from the block set that my best friend, Kendra, and I used to play with back in the day. I chose this because I want to be more like her. I want to grow in my ability to connect. Although we're both dedicated to our community, Kendra embodies it in a way that I aspire to. I want to move away from being so arrogant. I hope The Village can provide me the space to change."

"Well enough. Now, onto the Treasured Gift," Axel said. With this statement, The Villagers lined up shoulder to shoulder, with Maurice closest to Dom, reaching his hand out.

Dom felt awkward handing Maurice a picture of himself. The slight recoil from Maurice as he realized what the item was seemed to indicate something similar. The framed photo was passed down the line—Nille, Francis, Charles, Axel—and placed on the pedestal.

"I'm grateful that you all kept Maurice alive." His throat started to feel scratchy. "This is the last image my family had of him. It's the way I pictured him most often for five years. I now have a better understanding of why you stayed," he said, directly to Maurice, who avoided his look. "I just want you to remember all the people out there who love you." Maurice kept his head down in silence. His shoulders heaved incrementally higher with each breath.

"We will cherish this gift," Axel said. "Finally, please hand over the Treasure Lost."

Anticipating the burning, Dom had taken his diploma out of its frame and rolled it up just like the dummy one that was passed to him on stage at the graduation ceremony. "I have here the paper that symbolizes my old way of thinking. I'm nowhere near unlearning everything I need to in order to be an effective healer, but letting go of what I thought of as a grand accomplishment will light my path forward."

This time, Maurice didn't flinch when handed the scroll; instead, he gripped it tight, crumpling it in the middle. "Bullshit..." he muttered, as he passed the diploma down. Nille's eyes met Dom's, filled with the question of what Maurice's reaction was about.

Axel ignited a lighter, put it to the edge of the paper, then dropped the rapidly burning material into the metal bowl below. She stepped forward, arms out wide. "The first part of the initiation is now fin—"

"No!" Maurice broke from the line. The other three, wanting to maintain the atmosphere of the ceremony, moved only their eyeballs amongst each other, trying to discern what was happening.

Axel's glare seared into Maurice. "Why have you interrupted the ceremony?"

"Forgive me," Maurice bowed his head slightly. "But this is what I knew would happen. He isn't ready to fully commit." He went behind Axel and picked up his Senior Day photo. He marched toward Dom, shoving the photo so close it almost touched his nose. "*This* is what you need to let go of. You're still too focused on yourself and what you went through after I left. I'm not this person anymore. Until you understand that, you won't be able to put The Village before your own needs." He turned swiftly on his heel.

"Wait!" Dom was barely up out of his chair before it happened. In what felt like slow motion, he watched Maurice throw the photo into the growing fire. "That's the only one!" Fighting the urge to reach into the fire, he watched the memory of who his cousin was fade away.

"How could you do that?" Dom asked, almost bumping foreheads with Maurice.

Maurice grabbed him by the shoulders to put distance between them. "Stop. Just stop and accept it. You have to understand that this is the way things are going to be."

Axel had been standing by, not reacting to the commotion between the cousins. "While I'm disappointed by the lack of respect for the ceremony, Maurice has made himself clear. These are the terms that have been set for you. Do you still accept?"

Everything felt tangled inside, but he saw no other way forward. It was this or lose Maurice forever. And potentially his community. "Yes." He sat back in the chair.

"We will now move on to the naming portion of the ceremony." Axel waved her hand to have the other members follow her out of the room. "When we return, we will bid goodbye to Freedom Hall."

"So, he has no trial?" Maurice interrupted again. "We were all tested."

Axel tapped her foot. "He has done enough for us thus far to prove his loyalty. Do not question the ceremony again." They all left in a single file line.

Waiting, Dom watched the smoldering remains begin to lose their orange glow in the bowl. Tears welled, fighting to release.

After a few minutes, the rhythmic thump of a hand beating on the canvas of a drum began from somewhere out of sight. The echo was joined by the soft marching of feet. From around the corner, The Village reemerged.

Charles led the way, hitting the djembe drum tucked under his arm. Dom knew it was Charles from his height and hair, but a metallic mask covered his face. The other four trailing behind him in step with the drum, also wore masks. Nille's and Francis' were made of colorful cloths, while Axel's and Maurice's were wooden, painted with various colors. The kaleidoscope of masks also bore combinations of shining beads and crowns of feathers. They looked similar to the images he had seen of Carnival celebrations, but in this setting, they were more imposing, setting off anxiety inside him. They circled around Dom, the drumming and marching coming to a stop with a final loud smack of the djembe.

Axel again took the lead in the proceedings. "You will leave here today different than you came. Most importantly in value and mission, but also in name. Tell us what we shall call you."

The various books Francis had introduced Dom to had given plenty of options of names to choose from. So many brave and unsung heroes of resistance and liberation that were lost to history, deserving of being recognized by taking on their name. However, as he had contemplated the decision, he realized he had something of his own to reclaim. For so long, he was embarrassed by his full name and the implications baked into it. It was time for him to stop turning away from who he was so he could become something more.

"I will be known as Free."

"It must be something in your blood," Axel said, looking over at Maurice. "We gave your cousin an exception since he shared a name with someone who resisted and fought back against his oppressive conditions. Your name, however, has no parallel. Was there no one in our entire history that you could put above yourself? I fear Maurice may be right about your selfish nature."

Talking to her mask felt like he was talking to himself, which may have given him the bravery to speak up. "From the time you first explained what The Village was, you emphasized its evolution. Not all members are descendants of maroons, not all Village hubs even operate in the same way. You said that there was strength in this fluidity. Why can't I be granted another exception in order to embrace a part of me I've rejected for so long?"

She paused, seemingly in deep thought, but hard to tell through the mask. "I will accept this." A short grunt came from Maurice's mask. "You seem to have put lots of thought into this decision. It's a little on the nose, but as the newest member of The Village, you are now Free." The drumming started up again with a different rhythm, the surrounding stomping matching it. Axel placed her fist in front of her mask, which had a small opening at the mouth. She blew forcefully, sending a red powder pluming into his face.

Before he could react, he felt its effects taking hold. The rhythmic stomping lulled him into a trance as the masks around him came to life. It was a pleasant experience; no fear ran through him. He felt connected to the unknown number of others who had gone through the same ceremony. Physically and mentally lighter, he was Free.

CHAPTER
TWENTY-FOUR

The image of Maurice's burning portrait ran through his mind again. The previous night's ceremony, while still significant, felt incomplete without his cousin's full approval. He needed to figure out how to gain his trust. What he was about to do would probably set that goal back, but it couldn't wait. He knew the other Villagers' paranoia about being exposed would have kept them from supporting his idea.

Free leaned against the rail of the front porch of Kendra's house like he had on countless occasions growing up, waiting for her to come outside.

She came to the door in her bonnet, shielding her eyes from the late morning sun. "Hey." They had been texting and even spoke face-to-face once in the past month, yet an awkward energy could still be felt between them.

"Sorry, didn't know I'd be waking you up," Free said.

"It's all good. I needed to get up anyway. What's up, Dom?" She stepped out of the house to stand by him on the porch.

He paused for a moment, wanting to tell her to use his "new" name. He would have to wait and find a way to explain why without telling her about The Village. "I need your help with something. It's kind of a big deal."

She sighed and crossed her arms. "What did you do?"

"No, it's not like that. I'm asking you for help because you have the knowledge to come up with the right solution. Parkside's in trouble."

Kendra raised an eyebrow, looking annoyed. "What do you mean? There's always something going on. I think that little girl they found in an alley was from around here. You don't know something about that, do you?"

Free spaced out, battling with the grief in his heart, knowing that today should have been another session with Jasmine. "That's not what I came to talk to you about, but...yeah. Jasmine. She was one of my clients."

Kendra's mouth dropped. "Oh my god, Dom. I can't even...This city is so fucked up. I can't imagine what her parents are going through. Have you talked to them?"

Free shook his head. "Can't. I got fired Friday."

"Wait, what? What's going on, Dom?"

Free took a deep breath to organize his thoughts. "That's what I'm here to explain. Remember the drone and the scooter?"

"Yes, I remember my car getting dive-bombed and a bunch of kids almost getting run over. I think about throwing my phone every time one of Atlasal's ads pops up on my feed."

Free rubbed the back of his neck. "Yeah, well, I found out that those two events were connected."

"Dom. I'm gonna need you to get real specific because you're hurting my head right now. What are you talking about?"

He fumbled with his phone, taking it out of his pocket. It took three times to enter the correct passcode his hands were shaking so much. He felt confident at this point that Nille was not monitoring his phone, but what he did was still risky. Not only had he snuck pictures of Atlasal's sales projections and blueprints, he was about to reveal them to Kendra. To him, it made sense that the only way they could stall the plans at this point was to go public before Atlasal took control of the narrative, making their expansion seem like a natural progression.

"Here, look at this." Free handed Kendra his phone, explaining while she swiped through the photos. "They're all working together. Atlasal, New Horizons, the mayor; the whole city! They're literally selling us out."

Kendra's eyes narrowed. "Slow down. Tell me exactly what I'm looking at."

Free broke down Atlasal's entire plan.

"Shit...How do you know this is real?"

"Look! These pictures are from my CEO's laptop. That's where I got this info." It was close enough to the truth. He wanted so badly to mention the help he got from Maurice and The Village.

"That's why they fired you? For snooping through the boss's stuff?" Again, details aside, it was mostly true. "So, they know you have this, then."

"I'm not sure. Maybe. Look, that doesn't matter." Free took his phone back. "Whether they do or not, the clock is ticking. Atlasal may be early in the process of securing land, but if we don't act, Parkside is going to start changing before we know it."

"Okay, so the info's legit. Why am I the only one that can help you?"

"You're not the only one. It's going to take everyone in our neighborhood. And you can bring them together. You've shown me that your connection to this place, our home, is an invaluable strength."

A brightness seemed to return to Kendra. Free wanted their friendship to be normal again. Putting his ego aside was the first step.

"Well, it's nice to know I haven't been wasting my time with all these community programs." She gave a soft smile. "It's gonna take a lot of planning to stop a billion-dollar company, but I know I'm not gonna just sit back and watch them destroy our home. Let's do this."

THEY TOSSED IDEAS BACK AND FORTH OVER LUNCH before heading to an art studio Kendra frequently worked at.

"This is how I do my best thinking." She set up an easel and began painting aimlessly. "It opens my mind up."

A swirl of colors amassed as she continued brainstorming until she stopped suddenly, holding her paintbrush up in the air. "I got it! The Labor Day back-to-school celebrations will be a perfect setting. One of them is happening right where we had the block party. There's going to be so many people from Parkside there, we can start spreading the word there. Warn them about what's coming. Maybe some pamphlets or something? Or maybe keep it word of mouth until we know how many supporters we have."

That still left a couple weeks for New Horizons and Atlasal to get ahead if they knew he had their plans. Free wanted immediate action. "I think we should leak the plans online first. Get people's attention. If they already know what's going on, Labor Day can be when we bring people together with a more specific plan."

"Won't that just tip Atlasal off? And it will probably land you in trouble too."

"They already have the advantage by being a huge company with the city on its side," Free said. "We need to control the narrative. Putting their plan out online is the only way for us to get ahead of them." The same way Kendra was convinced by seeing the concrete information he'd uncovered, Free figured it was the quickest way to get others in the neighborhood onboard with coming together to fight back.

Kendra nodded slowly as she thought about it. "We both have enough followers for it to spread fast. To be safe though, let's drop the docs on a burner account and then we'll repost them." She tilted her head, staring at the swirls painted in front of her. "I feel like it's still going to be tough to plan something impactful by Labor Day."

Free gave her a determined look. "A wise woman once told me that this place and its people can't be separated." A smile came to her face. "Once people understand what's on the line, they'll want to do something about it."

They were both right. They reposted Atlasal's sales charts and blueprints to their social media accounts as they left the art studio. Their small corner of the Internet quickly caught fire. Their DM notifications didn't stop buzzing for the entire walk back to Kendra's house. There was outrage, skepticism, despair, a concession from Nate that "gentrification was gonna get us sooner or later," and questions about what to do.

"This is crazy," Kendra said. "We really started something." She showed him her screen, displaying a message she'd just received. It was from a local news reporter.

Can you confirm that these documents are legit? I'd like to talk to you about a potential story.

"What should I do?"

"We can't talk to the media about this," Free answered. "Let them think what they want. We know the threat is real, so we have to focus on the people in Parkside first. Let our actions speak." Between his now non-stop messages, a call from an unknown number came through.

Kendra saw his screen light up. "Careful, that could be someone from New Horizons. I'm sure the posts have made it to them too."

"Yeah, you're right," Free lied, declining the call while knowing who it really was. He scrolled through his messages. "It looks like we've got a lot of people already onboard. Let's keep this momentum and pick a day and place for people to meet up before Labor Day."

"Okay. I'll have a community-saving plan ready by then," Kendra replied. Her voice shook, her sarcasm enveloped in fear.

"You know better than me that people don't need saving. They just need to be shown the power inside them." He hurried off, waiting for Maurice to call him again. When his phone buzzed, he waited until the fourth ring to answer, anticipating the heat Maurice was going to give him.

"What. The. Fuck, Dom!"

As much as Free wanted to assert the use of his new name, he chose to stay silent.

"What made you think putting this shit out on the Internet was a good idea? Atlasal is a global company. This is going to be everywhere soon." Maurice's voice came in loud even with the phone held half an arm's length from Free's ear.

"Exactly! I don't get why outing them is a bad thing. A little public pressure might help. Why does everything have to be a secret with you guys?" Free grimaced at his mistake.

"You guys? You're one of us now, right, *Free*? This move of yours jeopardizes us. And I saw that Kendra posted this stuff with you. Even only her knowing puts us at risk. Now that Atlasal knows their plans got out, they're going to go through all their systems and could trace our hacks."

"Chill out, Maurice. You know Nille is better than that. She said way back that there's no way they can trace anything back to us. And Kendra's an asset, not a risk. You gotta trust us." He hung up, trying not to let his own doubts surface.

CHAPTER
TWENTY-FIVE

Free stood next to Kendra at the front of the group assembled, looking out at all the people they managed to bring together. So many showed interest in opposing Atlasal that they had to hold the meeting in an empty warehouse. This was the Parkside he knew. Elders on down to school-age kids gathered amongst each other, eager to find out what to do about the situation their neighborhood found itself in. Free spotted Nate and Britney in the mix along with many other faces he'd known since he was a kid.

Though his parents didn't know about the meeting, the leaked Atlasal info had made the local news along with details about how it got out. When they called him to ask why he spread the info, he dodged responsibility by saying he only shared it because it had to do with his job. The timing wasn't great, but he also told them about getting fired. They were disappointed, feeling he was creating a mess for himself. Something about being a disgruntled employee. Unfortunately, things would have to get messier to thwart Atlasal.

"You ready?" he turned to Kendra. She gave him an approving nod. Cupping his hands around his mouth, he shouted, "Okay, everybody! Listen up!" The group quieted down to a few murmurs, attention shifting to the two who called them there.

"Thank you all for coming here this morning," Kendra said, wringing her hands together while rocking back and forth.

Free gave her a soft nudge with his elbow. "You got this," he said so only she could hear.

Kendra rubbed her hands against her thighs and took a deep breath. "As you all know, Dom and I called you here for a reason. Parkside is being targeted by one of the fastest growing corporations in the world. Atlasal is trying to—going to—push us out of the way as they continue chasing more and more money. We're not going to let them do that."

Some heads nodded along with a few affirmative "mmhmms."

One voice near the back of the group echoed, "How can we stop them? They got the city on their side. Ain't nothing we can do."

Free craned his neck to see the woman who'd spoken up. She stood hunched over a walker, a little girl providing extra support. He answered her, "It's an uphill battle for sure. I wish we could have found out about this before Atlasal had the city's support, but we have to do the best with what we have. Like we've always done around here."

The little girl whispered to the woman, relaying his words. The woman didn't say anything back, only shifting her stance slightly. The little girl put an impatient hand on her hip, perhaps communicating for her grandmother that Free's response was not convincing.

Kendra took a step forward. "We have each other. Right now, our best bet is showing Atlasal and the city the truth about who lives here. That this is our space. We get overlooked by every system in Selton, but without us the city wouldn't be what it is. And we know that."

A handful of people nodded.

"Labor Day is around the corner," Kendra continued. "We'll be able to make a big statement at the back-to-school event on Randolph Road, but that won't be the end of our campaign. We have to be in this for the long run. And we have to do this together, with shared goals. To start brainstorming ideas, I'm going to break us into groups—"

The middle of the crowd started to budge and jolt. People stepped to the side as Nate squeezed his way through to the front. "Hold up. You might want to see this first." He handed Free his cell phone.

On the screen, Free read a social media post made by Atlasal announcing that Miranda Webb was coming to

Selton City to speak at Parkside's back-to-school event. Of course. She was going to be in town already to meet the winner of New Horizons' competition. Why not co-opt a community event to push a corporate narrative? It was quite the move.

Atlasal's post acknowledged the leaked information, offering to "start a conversation" about what their expansion meant for the community they "served and cared for" through their partnership with New Horizons. It read less like an apology and more like a public launch for the expansion plan.

"It looks like Atlasal is pulling out all the stops," Free said. He read the post out loud. "Miranda Webb is coming right to our doorstep." Reactions pulsed through the crowd as the implications of one of the country's most famous entrepreneurs coming to speak in their neighborhood settled in.

As he scanned the crowd, one man wearing a yellow bandana on his head did not seem to be as unsettled as the rest by the announcement. In fact, he stared straight back at Free, a cold look on his face. Maneuvering to get a better look, he recognized who it was. It was Francis. The Village wasn't going to let him continue his rogue plan without keeping eyes on him. Free received a text explaining Francis' demeanor.

Now do you see why the leak was a bad plan? This is why we make decisions together.

The energy in the crowd had shifted significantly. Free needed them to trust that even with this new element, they could succeed in making their voices heard. "I'm sure you all heard about the girl they found in an alley recently. Jasmine." A hush went through the crowd. Kendra placed her hand lightly on his forearm. "I don't know what to say about it other than I'm hurt. It feels like a betrayal by our city that someone so young could lose her life in that way. And they're betraying us again with this Atlasal situation. This is our home. We should feel free here, not used and discarded."

Kendra looked up at him with a proud expression and mouthed, *Okay, Freedom!*

She said to the crowd, "Now, we know Miranda is going to draw a lot of...outsiders from all across the city. We may have to switch up tactics, but having a bigger audience might work in our favor. We're gonna need to get creative to put something together quickly. Which is perfect because creativity is kinda my thing."

SEPTEMBER

CHAPTER
TWENTY-SIX

Free woke up feeling uncertain. Despite all the preparation, there was no way to know how the day would go. As he got closer to Kendra's house, he began to get confirmation that today would be different.

Cars he'd never seen before lined the street. A steady stream of them came up and down the block slowly, looking for places to park. People who were identifiably not from the neighborhood milled about, some looking down at their phones to guide them in the direction of Randolph Road. He knew most of them had never been to Parkside, or at least never got out of their cars there. Miranda wasn't scheduled to speak for a few hours, but people clearly didn't want to miss a chance at seeing her up close. He zipped up a lightweight jacket and picked up his pace.

Kendra was standing outside when he arrived at her house. She shook her head, looking at the people already intruding on their neighborhood. "This is exactly how this place is going to look if Atlasal pushes us out. Nope, I'm not cool with it. At all."

"Agreed. Are the canvases ready?" Free asked.

Kendra opened a text message. "Yup, they're in position. As we thought, there's a security presence on the ground."

Free nodded. "Okay, let's wait inside until it's time. I'm tired of all these stares already, like we don't live here."

When they arrived at Randolph Road around noon, they were met with a massive crowd. Sidewalk to sidewalk, people stood jammed next to each other. Free thought the street had been packed at the block party, but this was something else. Certainly, there had never been a crowd with such a mix of people. Atlasal was strategic if nothing else. Invite the people who typically neglect this part of the city into one of its significant spaces, and suddenly the current residents hold less of a claim on it. It didn't even resemble a back-to-school celebration anymore.

He got an adrenaline rush as they squeezed into the mass of bodies, knowing all their supporters were interspersed in the crowd waiting for the moment they had prepared for. People jostled about for the best view of the stage assembled at the end of the street. Complaints about when Miranda was coming out flew back and forth.

A few yards ahead, a screen-printed image on the back of a t-shirt stopped him in his tracks. A picture of Jasmine's smiling face with *Heaven's Newest Angel* printed above it seemed to look directly at him. He began to drift toward whoever was wearing the shirt, trying not to lose sight of Jasmine again. As he stepped up on the curb to get around a cluster of people, he was quickly bumped back down. Turning, he flinched at the presence of a plain-clothes cop, Selton Police Department badge flashing at his hip.

"Gotta keep the sidewalk clear. Safety hazard," the officer said, dryly.

"My bad," Free responded. Looking around, he spotted a couple of uniformed officers. He wondered how many more plain-clothes were dispersed throughout the crowd. He told Kendra to keep her head on a swivel.

They struggled one last time to get as close to the stage as possible. Still around thirty feet back, the crowd began to roar. Graphics flickered onto the screen on stage. Stock aerial shots of Selton City intermingled with scenes of people walking down busy streets. Free was reminded of the marketing video shown at New Horizons on his first day. A woman in the video stopped in front of a sleek modern building, looking up to the company name fixed to the façade: Atlasal. Cheers rang out as a trite EDM soundtrack ushered Miranda Webb to the stage.

She came forward, smiling brightly and waving both hands to the crowd like she was in front of a talk show studio audience. At the back of the stage, Free spotted the bun-wearing driver standing with his arms crossed. His lips moved slightly as he put a finger up to his ear.

Beginning to wave off the cheers, Miranda removed the microphone from the stand at the front of the stage. "Thank you, thank you. I appreciate the warm welcome." The clapping and screaming diffused as she placed the mic stand behind her, making room to walk back and forth. "I'm so pleased to see such a huge turnout from the people of Selton City!" Whoops and cheers leapt from the crowd. "I decided to come here on short notice, but I'm not surprised in the least. The energy of this city is one of the main reasons Atlasal chose to do business here."

Free scoffed at the lies.

"I know we have a lot to talk about. That's why I came here myself. While I don't support how the news got out to you all, I do promote honesty in all our company's practices."

Free and Kendra gave each other side-eyes. "You think this is all her, or does she have the worst speech writer ever?" Kendra asked.

Free shook his head. "Either way, she believes it." Far to his left, he saw a trio of people who were part of their group, all with similar disgusted looks on their faces.

"Atlasal is seeking to be a partner with this community. We started our relationship with Selton City by offering enhanced mental health care through our Haven program because we wanted to be of service to those most in need. As that relationship grows stronger, we need to hear your voices. So, think of this event today as the first of many conversations. Over the next few months, Atlasal will be launching a series of what we're calling community cafés, events where there will be opportunity to engage in dialogue about what else we can bring to our work in this city."

Free heard a groan somewhere behind him. Their group had been instructed not to boo at anything they heard from Miranda, so as not to draw untimely attention. There was no denying the absurdity of her statements though. It was clear she was not considering stopping Atlasal's expansion. And she had yet to mention Parkside specifically. By talking about the city broadly, she was side-stepping the intentionality of the company's plans. Hosting "community cafés" all over the city would only serve to drown out the needs of Parkside residents.

"I'm really excited to build stronger connections with you all. To talk some more about what this relationship building will look like, I want to bring out somebody I recently got to know. This person has been doing great work in the community, excelling at making transformational impact through the use of our health care technology. Come on out, Louis!"

A wave prickled down Free's body as he stared at the stage, wide-eyed. Of course, Louis had been in position to win the competition at New Horizons. What was so unexpected was that he would allow himself to be used as a pawn in Atlasal's scheme. Louis wasn't from Parkside, but he had to understand the danger of what the company's expansion would mean for the people.

Those concerns seemed nowhere present on Louis' beaming face as he walked out next to Miranda. She handed him the mic and stepped off to the side. "Thank you, Ms. We—Miranda. Hey, what's goin' on Selton!" The crowd clapped politely, but clearly wanted Miranda to be the center of attention again as soon as possible. "My name's Louis and I'm a therapist at New Horizons. Over the past few months, I've been lucky enough to see the amazing benefits of using Atlasal's virtual reality mental health care program, Haven. I could go on forever about the amazing product Miranda and her team have created."

"That's the guy you told me about before?" Kendra asked.

A nudge to his side shook him out of his shocked state. "Uh, yeah. He was skeptical of Atlasal at first, but clearly got sucked into the hype."

"We should act now," she said. "The crowd isn't too interested in him, so our message will be heard loud and clear."

"I, I don't know..." Free remained transfixed by Louis. The feeling of treachery was potent.

"From talking with Miranda, I know that her desire to support our city is genuine," Louis continued. "We shouldn't turn away from someone willing to use their resources to better our community." Miranda placed her hands over her heart in thanks.

"This guy..." Kendra nudged Free again. "Dom, we gotta do it now."

He felt glued to the ground.

Once Louis wound down his shameless endorsement, Miranda took the mic to speak again. "That was great! I know there's so many more of you like Louis out in the crowd today, and I can't wait to meet you and start working together."

The crowd erupted in more cheers. "She's gonna walk off the stage soon, Dom!" Kendra shouted through the noise around them. Again, no response. "Fuck it, it's now or never." She pulled her phone out and hit send on a drafted text.

Within seconds, it began. Six black-clad figures stood, three each on the top of two storefronts on opposite ends of the street. Large canvases unfurled over the front of the buildings, drawing everyone's attention as they flapped against brick and concrete. The applause for whatever Miranda was saying at the moment died down in a wave as people turned toward either side of the street. On the left, four faces were painted in a row, akin to a Black Mount Rushmore. The eyes of the faces were smudged out, giving the effect of hiding their identities. Across the top of the canvas read, PARKSIDERS

ARE REAL. On the right, a collection of hand and shoe prints filled the other canvas in a rainbow of colors. In a redux of the piece from the block party, a message was scrawled across the middle: WE'RE NOT GOING ANYWHERE.

Kendra's idea to use art as a form of protest had impressed Free from the jump. Her artistic skill not only defined the imagery used, but also what would make the most impact on the people present.

Murmurs and curious questions sounded throughout the crowd, but it was a clear statement from a man directly in front of him that snapped Free out of his stupor. "Probably some dumbass wannabe activists. Why don't they just let it go?" He laughed, flicking sweat around as he ran his hand through greasy hair.

Free looked over to Kendra just as she reached for her jacket zipper. He gave her a nod and did the same. As they turned to put their backs to the stage, Free saw men on the sidewalk trying to grab the canvases. From the build of some of them, he wondered if they were the other plain-clothes cops. The canvases were up too high to reach though, leaving the art as the backdrop to the continued demonstration.

Free felt like a synchronized swimmer as the others in their group made their presence known, also turning their backs to the stage. The crowd quieted down in pockets of confusion. A soft buzz rattled through as dozens of zippers came undone at once. Dropping their jackets to the ground, Free, Kendra, and all those they had gathered for the event began to chant in unison the words printed on the backs of their shirts.

"Back off Parkside!"

"Back off Parkside!"

"Back off Parkside!"

A mix of supportive cheers and annoyed jeers blended with the chant. There was some shoving off to the side, but everyone in the white t-shirts with bold, black lettering on the back held their ground. Phones came out all around to record the demonstration.

Miranda tapped the mic, trying to corral the situation. "Okay, let's get this under control."

It sounded like an order and apparently was, as Free saw one of the demonstrators get grabbed by the arm by a tall, blonde man with a buzz cut. Looking to his left, Free saw the officer who confronted him earlier begin to wade through the crowd toward him and Kendra. Just as Free was about to tell Kendra they should make a run for it, a hissing sound peaked over the commotion.

From multiple directions, clouds of red, black, and green smoke emerged from the ground. This wasn't part of their plan. Regardless, the smoke clouds created a necessary distraction. The crowd began to disperse at a pace that immediately felt dangerous. The clunk and high-pitched feedback of the microphone hitting the stage made Free look back. Miranda was being pulled off the stage by the driver.

Kendra tugged at his sleeve, shoving his jacket into his chest. "Come on let's go!"

Free took in the frantic look on her face. "Okay, okay. I need to do something first, though."

"What do you mean? Where are you going?"

"I won't be far behind."

Free weaved through streams of people heading in the opposite direction. A toddler cried in the arms of their parent. Feet away, an elderly man's glasses got knocked off in the commotion. Free couldn't slow down, pushing and squeezing until he reached the front of the stage, hopping up in one swift motion. He grabbed the microphone and looked out at the swarm trying to make its way off the street.

Peering through the twisting colors of smoke, Free swelled with an unfamiliar energy. The demonstration was supposed to get Atlasal's attention and let everyone know their expansion wouldn't be business as usual. He needed to make that clear. Emboldened by his community's display of resistance, he delivered his message.

"This is our village!"

Some stumbled as they looked back to see him on the stage. A number of those in Back Off Parkside shirts stopped in their tracks.

"Our people have always been a village, and we will protect what is ours! Today, we stand up with all the other villages willing to do the same!" Through the dissipating smoke, he saw a handful of men rushing toward the stage. Their shouts propelled their way to him like darts.

"Dom! Get outta there, quick!" About a dozen feet from the stage, Nate waved his arms at him.

Free dropped the mic, leapt from the stage, and followed Nate over a fence in an alleyway, a boost of adrenaline carrying him away from Randolph Road.

CHAPTER
TWENTY-SEVEN

RIOT.

The media was quick to categorize what had taken place. The softest language used described "a scary disturbance that interrupted what was supposed to be a positive moment for the city." National outlets picked up the story as well since Miranda Webb was supposedly put in harm's way.

Even worse, it was being reported that New Horizons had been vandalized not long after Miranda's speech was interrupted. As with the smoke canisters, the reported broken window and disheveled offices hadn't been part of their plan, but Free had an uncomfortable hunch who was responsible.

As night fell, he entered The Village hideout ready to explode. "Please, tell me you didn't break into New

Horizons!" All the Villagers were standing together, but Free's glare fell on Charles.

Charles held the eye contact. "Don't give me any more shit about—"

"Stop." Axel put a hand up. "We don't have time for this. Yes, we had to access the building in order to gather intel."

Nille held up a Haven headset. "It *was* Charles, for the record, but I'm the one that recommended it." Charles stepped toward her, but one snap of Axel's fingers brought him back to his position.

"Wait, what's going on?" Free crossed his arms. "This isn't what Kendra and I had in mind. Not the smoke, and definitely not breaking and entering. The way the cops are going to come down on Parkside now, it's only going to make people more afraid to fight back against Atlasal. Why did you steal the headset?"

"We had nothing to do with the smoke canisters. And deciding to put the spotlight on yourselves was your decision," Maurice said.

Free wanted to spit at the chastising remark.

"While we were here staying out of your stunt, our monitoring picked up something none of us were expecting," Maurice continued.

Axel raised an eyebrow at him. "Don't let fear undersell the threat we've uncovered," she stated.

Maurice dropped his head, sullen. "Just show him, Nille."

She waved Free over to her computer. "The security cameras on Randolph didn't have great views, but a lot of people were posting to social media during Miranda's speech. Proof that they were there, ya' know? One person's live video feed kept a good angle on the stage even when the smokescreen started. Right when Miranda got pulled off the stage, Francis spotted something."

She paused the video she'd brought up at the moment the driver came to take Miranda away from the unfolding disorder. What stood out to Free was seeing Louis' back as he was already running away, clearly unconcerned about the woman he was so willing to help destroy their community. Nille zoomed in on the driver's hand grabbing Miranda's arm. A click of the mouse enhanced the image, revealing details of the tattoo he had not been able to make out the first time he saw the man smoking outside of New Horizons. It was a five-pointed star with eyes under each point, only one of them open.

"Wait, I've seen that before," Free said, recalling the card that fell from Jasmine's pocket. He was so stunned by her death, he'd forgotten about it. His stomach felt queasy.

The room gasped collectively. Nille leaned back, looking sideways at him in surprise. "Where? You know what that is?"

Free shook his head, feeling like he was being scolded for seeing something he shouldn't have. "In my last session with Jasmine, she showed me a card some boy had given her with the same symbol on it. She was told it was a random logo the kid's brother designed. It seemed a little sketchy, but now I'm even more confused."

"A child gave her the card?" Francis asked. "Maybe he just found it and made up a story."

"There's too many connections for it to be a coincidence, Francis," Axel said. "It seems that they used her and then killed her."

"Who?" Free held back tears. "What's going on?"

"That star...is a Seeker symbol," Francis said. "For as long as The Village has existed, the Seekers have been trying to end it. They're also known as Star Gazers, hence the symbol, because their forebears learned that some of the enslaved used the stars as a guide to escape; so, they adopted the same tactic in order to track them down. Through centuries of hunting, their tactics have only become more horrendous."

Free was stunned. "Why didn't you tell me about the Seekers before?"

"It isn't something we discuss right away with new Villagers," Axel said. "The lurking presence of an enemy can distract newcomers from our core mission. But now that we know they are linked to Webb and Atlasal, we must face the problem head on."

"So, is Miranda a Seeker, then?" Free asked.

"No, she doesn't fit their criteria. Whether she knows the driver is a Seeker is another question. Regardless, they made their presence known through your client. They must have somehow figured out we were in contact with you. There's no other reason to do so."

"How could they know that?" Free asked.

"We're not sure yet, but we're going to keep looking into it," Axel answered. "I know there's a lot going through your head right now, but we can't afford any rash decisions. There's a target on your back not only from Atlasal and the police, but now the Seekers. We need you to lay low until we can get a handle on the situation. So, we are sending you on an assignment."

"An assignment? Can't this wait? I want to help track down the Seekers."

"No. Time is of the essence. And the delivery you'll be making will help." Axel nodded at Nille.

Pulling up another video, Nille explained, "Your spur of the moment speech at the end caught some attention." She hit play.

"This is our village. Our people have always been a village..."

"It seems your repeated reference to a 'village' sent a signal. We saw a message come up in this live video feed that stood out."

She paused the video with a comment on the screen that read: *Our Village is with you. Even if Atlasal makes you flee to the hills, you will survive.*

"The capitalized 'V'. The reference to the hills. It piqued our interest," she said.

The People of the Hills. Free recalled Axel mentioning the original name of The Village when he first met them.

"We reached out, using coded language only Villagers know and it turns out the commenter is a member of another hub. In the Caribbean." She turned to Axel.

"They want to help us," Axel said. "They picked up on the Seeker presence as well and think the Haven tech is a potential link. Apparently, they've had more recent run-ins with the Seekers and have seen them use advanced technology to their advantage. They have someone familiar with Seeker tech that wants a crack at the headset. That's why we had to acquire one. And you're going to bring it to them."

"Why not just mail it?" Free asked.

"Again, we're moving off the assumption the Seekers know we are here and they're tied in with Atlasal's interests." Axel responded. "We can never be too sure where a Seeker may be located. Trusting the mail is out of the question."

"And an airport is safer?" Free asked.

"I can handle TSA's systems long enough to get you through," Nille said. "Look, I'm just as upset as you. I would love to tinker with this headset, but I guess I'll trust our Village brethren."

Free pondered what was being asked of him.

"It's been a while since we've connected with another Village hub, especially internationally," Axel said.

"And you need to stay away from Selton for a while until things cool off, anyway."

Maurice stepped in. "Since you're so bent on raising our profile, we're trusting you to ensure this connection is worth our time."

"What he means is," Axel interjected before Maurice could go on a rant, "is that your message may have stood out to more than just this hub. This trip will serve as somewhat of a test run in case other hubs make contact with us. While we are all one, we have to be strategic about how we work together."

The struggle against Atlasal was already more complicated than Free could have imagined. He needed to find out who Jasmine's murderers were and what bigger plans they had. They had infiltrated his life, and it was time to do some digging of his own.

"I HAVE TO GO."

"Now? There's all this heat on us and you're just going to leave?"

"It'll only be for a week or so, I promise. Then I'll be right back to stand with you. I trust that you can take care of things until then."

Kendra looked at him, analyzing him from the inside out. He knew what she was thinking.

"It's different this time. I'm doing this for all of us."

ACKNOWLEDGMENTS

Thank you to all the family and friends who have supported me on my journey as an independent author thus far.

Thank you to my fiancée, Samantha, for all the support you've given me including your feedback on the various iterations of the book cover, character names, and my impulsive merch ideas.

Thank you to my beta readers, Kevin and Besu. You both provided valuable feedback that helped flesh out several aspects of the story and push my craft further.

Thank you to my editor, Megan, for helping me sharpen my sentences and boosting my confidence in the story I created.

Thank you to those who bought my first book, *Tales of a Black Therapist*, showing me that my work was valuable and motivating me to continue writing (although I would have continued even if no one bought it).

Thank you to my ancestors, both ancient and recent, for surviving and giving me the opportunity to share the strength in our stories.

Thank you to you, the reader. *Where We Are Free* is the first book in a planned duology and the entry point to many more stories involving The Village and all its members. I hope you have become as curious as I am to see where these characters' journeys take them.

Lastly, a special, singular thank you goes to my mom whose love of reading inspired my own and unknowingly put me on the path toward becoming an author. In November 2024, two days after I finished the first draft of *Where We Are Free*, she passed away suddenly. It has been a tremendous loss to process, but I cherish all the moments I had with her and the memories that will remain, only one of which was her excitement at being able to hold and read my first book. I love you and I miss you, Mom.

ABOUT THE AUTHOR

CHRIS GAMBLE IS A MENTAL HEALTH PROFESSIONAL in Washington, D.C. He uses what he's learned through his work to craft stories that heal and liberate, with the ultimate goal of shifting how people understand mental health and the systems that impact it. He started his own publishing company, Blank Passage, to house his writing and become an educational hub for how to write about mental health with accuracy and care. You can keep up with future developments by visiting www.blankpassagellc.com and following him on Instagram @ chris_thecounselor.